THE MADNESS OF IDA MAE

THE MADNESS OF IDA MAE

and other stories of love,
murder & misfits

CHRISTINE BAGLEY

Author Photo Credit: Peter Bagley

I wish to acknowledge the following publications where some of these stories first appeared in earlier versions:

Best New England Crime Stories: Stone Cold ("The Elevator")

Briar Cliff Review ("With Grace")

Best New England Crime Stories: Bloodroot ("Valhalla")

Untoward Magazine ("Keeping Abreast")

Best New England Crime Stories: Landfall ("Dear Ruth")

Bryant Literary Review ("The Madness of Ida Mae")

FICTION ON THE WEB, UK ("Scapegoat")

First edition

ISBN: 978-1-68512-714-5

Cover art by Level Best Designs

This book was professionally typeset on Reedsy.
Find out more at reedsy.com

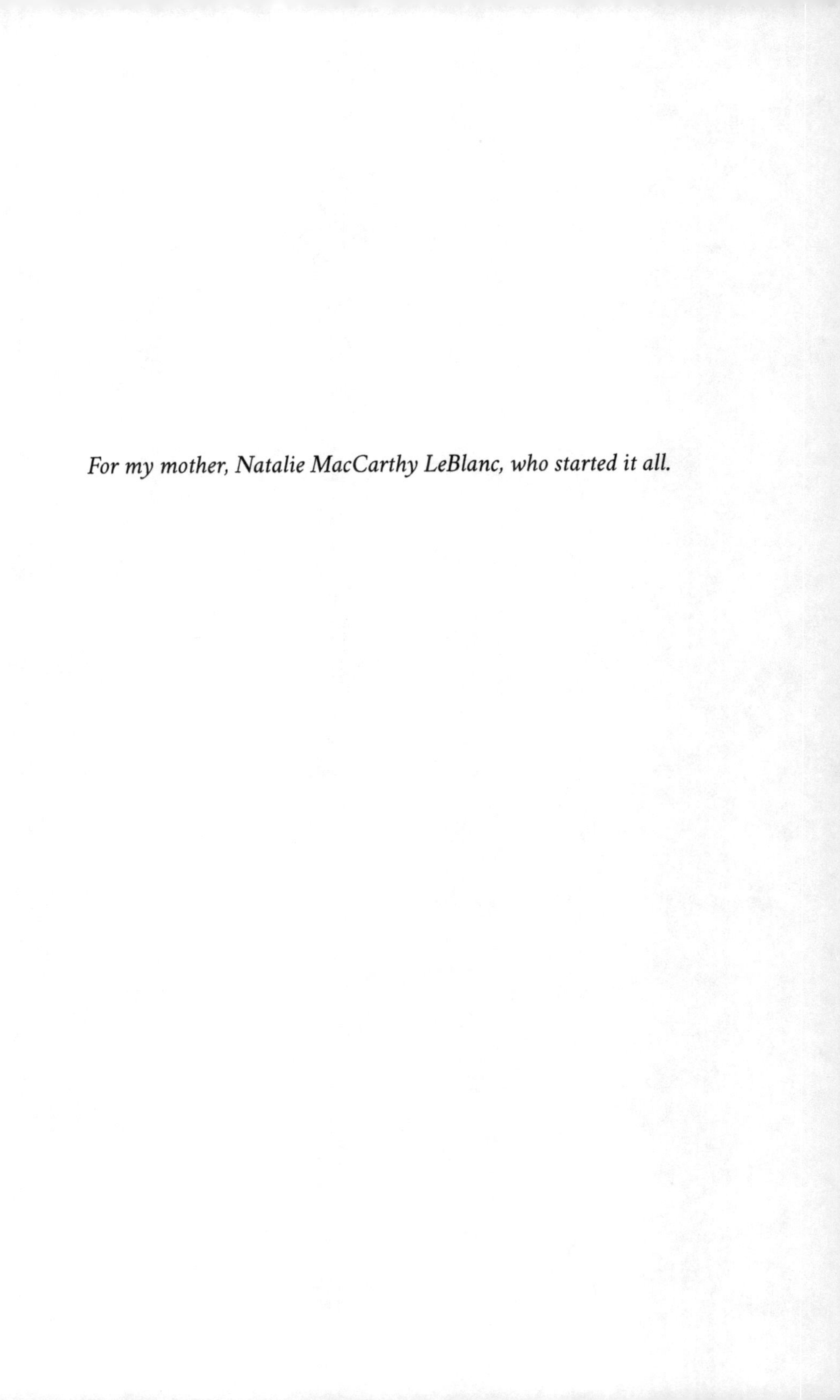

For my mother, Natalie MacCarthy LeBlanc, who started it all.

"When you read a short story, you come out a little more aware and a little more in love with the world around you."

– George Saunders

Contents

Praise for The Madness of Ida Mae

"Christine Bagley dazzles in her range of genres, quirky characters, humor and wit, and compassion for the foibles of men longing for love or legacy, and women hanging on to the little they have. In language graceful as well as original, she explores loss, desperation, and redemption in characters we might never meet but deeply understand."—Susan Oleksiw, author of the Anita Ray mystery series

"*The Madness of Ida Mae* is a wonderful eclectic collection of short fiction from Christine Bagley. Her stories encapsulate revenge, love lost, murder, and madness. Brilliantly written and imaginative!"—Bruce Robert Coffin, international bestselling coauthor of The Turner and Mosley Files

The Elevator

It was Friday night, and everyone had ducked out early because of the impending Nor'easter. From my office window at Boston Research, I saw the first flakes fall like white confetti from the street lamp. I was a research analyst and needed to finish a report because I'd had a manicure at lunch, then spent the afternoon emailing blonde jokes with my cousin, Claire. My favorite was the blonde who got all excited because she finished a jigsaw puzzle in six months when the box said two-four years.

I didn't leave until almost seven o'clock and before I took off, I went into my boss's office and chose a pair of purple pumps that she kept in a shoe rack under her desk. Shoes are like goldfish to a cat for me, and she had them in every color, good ones, too, like Tod's and Stuart Weitzman's. I put them in a plastic bag and shoved them in my tote bag to be returned early Monday morning before she found out what a weasel I can be. I just can't help myself sometimes. It's like I've got a naughty gene in my DNA. Even though I know it's wrong, I go ahead and do it anyway.

I walked down the hall toward the elevator. The building was empty, and only the red EXIT signs and a few auxiliary lights were on. Standing in front of the elevator, I pressed the button with my freshly polished forefinger (Mulberry Mojo, in case you wanted to know). Normally, I don't take the elevator because I'm claustrophobic and have serious anxiety issues. But I was going to miss the train if I didn't hurry. I was thinking about going home to Sebastian and watching a movie, *Where the Crawdads Sing*, I think it was, trying to enjoy the simpler things since we'd gotten back together. Maybe make some popcorn.

Last year, we'd bought a home in Marblehead, near Devereux Beach. I grew up in Lynn, a diverse city with a scenic shoreline and a bad rep. We beach girls would lean on our elbows in skimpy bikinis and stare at Marblehead's coastline from Nahant Beach. We always thought people who lived there had made it in life. Either that or they'd inherited a truckload of money.

The doors opened, and I pushed the *L button on the panel. I tried to assume a blasé attitude, humming Sheryl Crow's *A Change Will Do You Good*, and pretending I wasn't afraid—one little bit. The elevator began its descent, and when it came to a hard stop, bouncing between the fifth and fourth floors, my stomach lurched. I pressed the alarm button. Nothing. I jammed it five more times. And then everything went dark and a small emergency light on the ceiling came on. My biggest fear had just been realized.

I'd just weaned myself off the anti-anxiety meds that my doctor prescribed after I was charged with assault. A cabbie had splashed me, so I'd thrown an apple at him, and he drove into a fire hydrant. The cops said I needed anger management classes. My doctor prescribed Klonopin.

Pawing frantically through my tote bag for my iPhone, I remembered I'd left it in my office on the charger.

"Help! Somebody—help me!"

I started feeling light-headed and slumped against the wall, taking deep breaths as I slid to the floor. I pulled my laptop out of its sleeve. My hands shook as I tried to get online but there was no wireless in the elevator. Huddling with my head between my knees, I started whimpering like a hungry infant.

"Is anyone out there?"

I didn't even recognize my hoarse, childlike voice. I wondered if someone aware of my phobia had done this to me on purpose, like Ray, the Plant Ops guy I'd complained about for not replacing the fluorescent light in my office.

An hour later, I was sitting on the floor in black tights and a bra. It felt like two hundred degrees, and I'd pulled a folder out of my briefcase to fan myself. I imagined myself diving naked into a snow bank. My coat, boots, sweater, and skirt were in a pile on the floor beside me like a rummage sale.

Naturally, my panic over getting a panic attack brought on a full-blown panic attack. I couldn't get enough air into my lungs and my mind was like a blender on puree.

I didn't care that my doctor had told me I couldn't die from a panic attack. She'd never had one. I know because I asked her. So, how could she know what it felt like? Well, I'll tell you, it's as if you're suffocating from the inside out and no one, I mean no one, can help you—okay?

I started panting as though I were in labor. After a few minutes, I settled down; minutes that seemed like hours. I felt a tremendous sense of relief when the panic attack was over, so much so that I started rationalizing my own death. People who were afraid of water ended up drowning. The person terrified of height falls out a window, and the one who's claustrophobic? DIES IN AN ELEVATOR!

I used to wonder how I'd die. Now I knew. I began to summarize my life over the past forty years, not surprised that my total was low in good deeds and high in bad behavior. If what I believed was going to happen, then I'd better atone for my wicked deeds before my demise. It would help me focus until my expiration and might allow me a pass to heaven, or at least limbo for a few years until I could ascend for good behavior. I would have to show remorse to receive absolution. I could do that. I really *was* sorry for a lot of the things I'd done.

I opened my laptop and started writing in a stream of consciousness, with no regard for how it would sound on the other end. I couldn't get on the internet, but my emails would be stacked up and ready to go—post mortem.

Although I debated starting with my husband, Sebastian, I felt I should warm up first before I got into real hot water.

I began with my son, who, although he was a first-class jerk sometimes, was the best thing I'd ever done, and I loved him more than life.

To my dear son, Aidan:

I'm stuck in the elevator at work, and everyone has gone home. You know I have anxiety issues, and I'm claustrophobic, so it will come as no surprise that the combination, in the end, has killed me. I want you to know how much I love you and what a good son you've always been.

You are the light of my life, and I'm so sorry that I told your girlfriend, Erin, that you cheated on her. That's why she broke up with you, Aidan. I said you were a born womanizer that you began flirting in the sandbox. You guys were too young to get serious anyway, and I truly think she was up to no good. She had that awful habit with her eyes, you know, the way she opened them real wide like she was going to kill someone and then rolled them around in her head so quickly you were never sure of her meaning? Anyway, please forgive me and put flowers on my grave on my birthday like a good son. It's May 9^{th,} in case you forgot.

 Love,

 Mom

The emergency light went out, and only a blue hue from the laptop screen lit the elevator. I looked around my eerie quarters, thinking that this was where it would all end, alone, confessing my sins on a laptop. I chewed my cuticles, biting off the new polish and spitting the chips out in the air while I thought of who should come next. I guess my sister. Oh boy.

Dear Lauren:

 I've always known you were Mom's favorite. But that doesn't matter now. By the time you read this, I'll be lying on a steel tray in the morgue. (I hope they use a nice shade of mauve on my lips and not too much powder, like they did with Nelly Thibodeau, remember?) Anyway, what I have to tell you is going to come as a shock. A few years ago, I told Mom that you were pregnant in high school and gave the baby up for adoption. Remember when you spent the summer at the Vineyard with Diane Delaney? I told her that's when you had the baby. Anyway, that's why she left you out of the will. Not because you were pregnant, Lauren, which you weren't, but because you lied to her, which you really didn't, but she didn't know that and wanted you to need her, which you would have had you been pregnant, which you weren't. If you aren't at the funeral, I totally get it.

 Love,

 Leyla

Lauren hated me anyway so this would give her even more reason to be glad I was gone. I thought about my best friend and hoped she understood the circumstances and forgave me. Anger is a terrible thing to hold on to.

Dear Karen:

By the time you read this, I'll be gone from this world. You have been the dearest friend a girl could have, and I want you to know that. But there's something I must confess, and that is that I had phone sex with your hubby, Noah. I'm sooo sorry, KiKi. Sebastian and I had split up, and I got drunk and called you. You were out, and Noah and I started chatting, and then one thing led to another. It was dumb I know but what an amazing imagination Noah has. Once he got going, I couldn't believe what I was hearing. He should really be a writer. Anyway, we've shared so much together. Remember the time we got high on Aidan's weed and called that cute waiter at Palmer's and told him we really liked his poached pears? You didn't deserve what I did to you, and I understand if you don't visit my grave.

Love,

LiLi

I was on a roll. It was starting to feel good, this atonement thing. The trouble was I had to pee. The next person on the list was my boss.

Dear Eleanor –

I'll make this short because I know you hate when I'm wordy. I'm dead. You'll need a replacement. I borrowed your shoes every weekend and returned them on Monday. I'm sorry. I fudged the figures on the report. I hope that makes up for wearing your shoes.

Regards,

Leyla

My bladder was about to explode, and I wondered how much longer I could hold on. But then I remembered that when you die, everything gets released from your body anyway, so what did it matter? This thought reminded me of my poodle, Afro. He would never receive this, but he deserved my regret anyway. I could feel the tears coming as the words blurred in front of me. What a total shit I was.

> *Dear Afro:*
>
> *As long as I'm atoning for my sins, I need to write to you, too. I know you'll never receive this, but you deserve an apology anyway. You were the most adorable little puppy in the world, but I just couldn't take the peeing, chewing, snapping, and barking anymore. Also, you had that awful smell, like fried poop and pineapple. I'm sorry I let you out in that parking lot on the Lynnway. I've thought about you a lot since then, and I truly regret what I did to you. Sebastian and Aidan still think someone stole you from the back yard, but you and I know better. My hope is that some old couple has taken you in and that they're providing you with the love they've missed from never having a child of their own.*
>
> *Love, your bitch mother*

I cried hard then, wailing like a banshee for all the selfish, shameful things I'd done. When I didn't have any tears left, I blew my nose and took a deep breath. It was time to write to my husband.

> *Dear Sebastian:*
>
> *By the time you read this, I'll have passed over. You see, I'm stuck in the elevator at work and will probably die soon. Before I leave this world however, I have to tell you that I love you I have always loved you, even though for the past five years every single thing you did got on my nerves. We all have our faults, Sebastian, but there's something that you should know that I cannot take to my grave. Remember when Alfonso Rodriguez was convicted of criminally negligent manslaughter in your mother's death? Well—it was me who orchestrated the whole*

thing. I hired Alfonso to deliver groceries to your mother's house, which included a jar of Vaseline, which he smashed on her front stairs just before she went to get the paper. I have to say he timed it perfectly. She never suffered. Into the air, she went and came slamming back down on that stone walkway she'd spent thousands on. But if we didn't get her inheritance, we were going to lose the house in Marblehead. She was a mean old coot anyway, Sebastian, you know that. She never gave Aidan anything in his entire life, not even a hug, even though she had more money than the Arabs. And the way I figured it, Alfonso being in prison got him a roof over his head and three squares. Plus, I promised him ten thousand dollars when he gets out. I just thought you should know the truth. Please have me cremated if it's easier.

Your loving wife,

Leyla

I was drained from the emotion I'd expended and felt myself sliding away. I wasn't in pain, and I had made my peace. It was up to a higher power now to decide my fate after death. Drifting into nothingness wasn't so bad, calmly and softly floating as if I was made of lavender chiffon. Ever so slowly, a mild current carried me off to oblivion.

Hours later, in the far-off distance of a jumbled dream sleep, I heard the elevator doors opening. I was still in my underwear when the fire chief kneeled down in front of me and asked if I was okay. I looked at my watch. It was two o'clock in the morning. I'd been in the elevator for seven hours. Then I looked down at my laptop. The wireless had kicked in, enabling Outlook to send six emails through the system to their recipients. The fire chief lifted me to my feet and wrapped my coat around me. Sobbing, I flopped onto the couch in the lobby. I had peed my pants, and the smell of urine permeated the air. I felt like the wretched waif who'd shamed the village.

As I sat there, I realized I could never go home. I had no family, no friends, not even a boss anymore. I'd burned all my bridges. The only thing I could do was go to a hotel for the night. Maybe tomorrow, I'd take out all the cash I had and fly to Mexico. With my fluent Spanish, I could work as a translator somewhere. I sat up straighter. Yes, that's what I'll do. But I'll need to change my appearance in case Sebastian sends the cops after me. I could dye my hair auburn and then get some green contact lenses. I've always loved auburn and the way the light turns it different shades of red. I'll make new friends, get a nice apartment overlooking the water. I'll be a better person. I swear I will. I'll stop lying. I won't steal or cheat ever again. And I'll never, ever get any pets that I can't take care of.

Well, maybe a bird. I don't know. Then, if it becomes a nuisance, I can open a window and let the little bastard out.

With Grace

Stephen clears his throat. "The plane's here."

I pick up my handbag with the gift inside—a small butterfly necklace that took me two hours to choose. I'd walked from store to store, wondering what would be appropriate. What do you buy for the child of your husband's affair with another woman, someone you just learned about three weeks ago? An American Girl doll to acclimate her to her new country? A locket to hold the picture of a mother who died in the bomb blasts in Ahmedabad?

My heart feels like a marching band as my eyes move down the line of people. I look toward the gate and try to imagine what she looks like. Her name is Sunita, and she's five years old. A young girl escorted by a flight attendant comes toward us, and I feel like I am seeing someone I know but can't remember how I know her. Then I realize I am staring at Stephen's blue eyes and cleft chin, and I'm shocked by the resemblance.

Sunita looks lost and vulnerable, and I feel conflicted by my anger toward Stephen and compassion for the child who is innocent in all of this. Stephen is watching me, and I force myself to remain impassive.

Sunita carries very little with her—a tiny suitcase and a light sweater. It is obvious that she's been crying, and a towel is wrapped around her waist. Stephen crouches down and says, "Hi, Sunita. I'm your father. Welcome to your new home."

I see the uncertainty in her eyes and think how different it would be if Sunita were a child from India we were adopting instead of a child of his adultery.

The attendant tells Stephen and me that Sunita has wet herself and needs to be changed. Stephen stands up and looks my way. I feel manipulated, knowing I will have to handle the situation, resenting this responsibility for his daughter so quickly. Stephen gives Sunita a half smile to reassure her, but she puts her head down and sticks her thumb in her mouth. I am embarrassed for the child I am unprepared to feel anything for.

"Come with me, Sunita," I say, trying to appear confident. I walk toward the restrooms and realize she's not keeping up with me. I stop and hold out my hand. Together, we walk down the wide corridor of Logan Airport, Boston's skyline, like a bar graph in the background. Sunita's hand is small, and she barely reaches my waist. Was her mother small, and did she have a red dot in the middle of her forehead? Had she worn colorful saris and thick black eyeliner? Was she ashamed that she'd slept with a married man and become pregnant?

* * *

In the ladies' room, I pass a woman diapering her baby and ask for a few wipes. Once inside the stall, Sunita covers her face and whimpers. I find a handkerchief in my pocketbook and hand it to her. While she dries her tears, I ask, "Do you speak English?"

She nods.

"You have a change of clothes in here, right?" I say, pointing to the small suitcase.

"Yes."

"Okay." I take a deep breath. "Let's get you changed."

Sunita looks away. This is the first test of my skills as a mother, yet I have no right to force her to do anything. But she smells of urine, and the crotch of her pants is soaked. I open the suitcase as the smell of eucalyptus and jasmine floats out. Each piece looks as if it has been ironed, and I picture a dark woman carefully packing the clothing. I pull out a pink long-sleeved T-shirt, dark pants, and underwear. Sunita huddles in the corner, sucking her thumb, watching me. I am struck again by her resemblance to Stephen, and I feel my heart squeeze.

"It's okay," I say softly. "I'm not going to hurt you. I'm just trying to help you." My face is flushed with the awkwardness of the situation and the confinement of the stall.

"Please, Sunita," I say.

She hears the urgency in my voice and moves obediently in front of me. I bend down and remove her sneakers, unsnap her pants, and pull them down along with her underpants. Sunita takes her feet out of the pant legs one at a time, still sucking her thumb. As gently as possible, I clean her, trying not to touch her any more than I have to. I slip on her underwear and pants, then pull her T-shirt over her head, careful not to catch it in the miniature hoop earrings.

"Better?"

Sunita bobs her head and looks relieved. I ask her to put her sneakers on and leave the stall to rinse my face with cold water. I think of Stephen outside waiting. I want to delay, make him nervous. Make him question if I am able to handle the situation. Am I impatient? Aloof? Or am I the great mother Stephen always said I'd be?

I gnaw on the cuticle of my right thumb, remembering my coldness toward him before leaving for the airport this morning.

* * *

"Grace?" he'd called, his voice strained, apologetic. "We have to leave now."

I was in the bathroom wiping my mouth with a facecloth after throwing up. Some people get migraines when they're stressed. I barf.

"Are you alright?" he'd asked, nearing the bathroom door.

I didn't answer.

"Can I do anything?"

"You already have," I murmured.

The misery in his voice angered me because he had brought this on himself—yet his anguish has become mine.

Sunita and I find Stephen across the terminal waiting. As he comes toward us, he bumps into a woman crossing in front of him. He takes Sunita's hand, and they walk ahead of me. I watch father and daughter and the empty space where a mother should be. I could have taken Sunita's other hand. But my feelings for them are complicated, and I'm unsure whether I can forgive him and raise his child from another woman.

* * *

Three weeks ago, I'd been brushing my teeth before bed. After shutting the bathroom light off, I saw Stephen sitting on the bed.

"Grace," he said softly. He had the same expression as when our Golden Retriever had been hit by a car, and I felt myself grow tense. "Do you remember when I went to Gujarat five years ago?" he asked.

I waited.

"While I was there, I had a translator," he said. His voice was so low it was hard to hear him. "Her name was Esha. Hindu pilgrims had been burned alive on a train bombed by a mob of Muslims. It was horrible, Grace, just horrible. Esha's entire family was killed," he continued. He'd put his hands on either side of him, grabbing the edge of the bed. "She was distraught…and…." He'd looked up at the ceiling and exhaled loudly. His face was drained, and I saw the panic in his eyes.

"And?" I whispered, knowing what he was going to say but making him say it anyway.

"I slept with her."

I sank down on the bed as far away from him as possible and stared at an oil painting: a tranquil scene on Martha's Vineyard, of morning sea mist hovering Menemsha Bight and the dark blue waters of the Atlantic. I remember wanting desperately to be in that painting and escape the scene in which I was now trapped.

"I'm so sorry," Stephen said, his voice cracking. But I kept staring at the picture, his voice like a television left on in the background. "You can't imagine what it was like over there," he went on. "For two months, there were gunshots all around us, car bombs, screaming and crying. For the first time in my life, I thought I was going to die." Stephen rose and walked around the bedroom, running his hands through his hair.

"Were you in love with her?"

"No," he'd said adamantly. "I *cared* for her. She was kind and laughed at the way I mispronounced the language. She was a great help to me in understanding the culture.

* * *

I lag behind them until we get to the car. Sunita sits in the backseat and Stephen places the suitcase beside her, carefully buckling her in. While he drives, he looks straight ahead with both hands on the wheel. He must see how much Sunita looks like him. Is he proud of that? I would be.

We head south of the city toward the Cape and the Islands. It is May and the trees are light green along the highway. Sunita is sucking her thumb and gazing out the window. When she realizes I'm looking at her, she pulls her thumb out and starts fidgeting with the seat belt. I look away, curious if Sunita is uncomfortable because of what happened in the ladies' room or because I have invaded the thoughts of her mother.

An hour later, we pull into the driveway of the house we've lived in for fifteen years. What started as a two-story colonial now has a sunken family room with floor-to-ceiling windows overlooking the lake, a master bedroom suite, a remodeled kitchen that belongs in *Architectural Digest*, a study, and an extra bedroom, a bedroom that was supposed to be for *our* child, and will now belong to Sunita.

Stephen turns the car off and puts his hand on my thigh.

"Grace."

"Don't," I say and open the door to get away from him. I hear him bang the steering wheel before I close the door, and I want to scream, "What right do you have to be angry?" But I don't want to upset Sunita. She turns and looks out the window at the house.

* * *

Stephen shows Sunita her bedroom while I start dinner.

As I peel potatoes, I look out at the circular garden in the front yard where the cornflowers, poppies, and hyacinths are in bloom. The deep blue color of the cornflowers reminds me of the woman at the airport who walked by in tight black pants and a deep blue blazer. Flawlessly made up, she wore stilettos, seemingly strong and confident, her white blonde hair in a chic blunt cut. I'd looked down at my faded jeans and sneakers and green sweatshirt with the words *Global Warming Isn't Cool* printed across the front. My hair is in a low ponytail, and I'd felt mousy in comparison, my self-esteem at an all-time low.

Stephen had once told me, "You don't need makeup or fancy clothes. You're one of those women who's naturally good-looking." Perhaps he'd grown tired of my natural looks and wanted something more exotic.

Stephen and Sunita come down the stairs and enter the kitchen. "We're going for a walk down to the lake. It's a nice place to read a book. Do you like to read, Sunita?" She nods as Stephen pulls her along. She turns to look at me, tilting her head as if to say, *are you coming, too?* At least she's conscious of not leaving me out.

I run water over the potatoes. Stephen seems to be adapting well, but of course that's what he does for a living, Head of Communications for UNESCO, able to manage crises in the midst of war and pandemonium, the peacemaker between fighting brothers, the one who became the father of the family after his own father passed away.

He should be the one not sleeping—he should be the one throwing up or crying in the middle of a store when, for one tiny moment, he forgets about the cheating, and when he does remember, it hurts even more.

As I cut off the top of the carrots, I try to keep from crying, ashamed, and infuriated by my vulnerability. I take the chicken out of the fridge and slam it on the counter. Before I wash my hands and roll the chicken in breadcrumbs, I remove my wedding ring and place it on the windowsill, the simple silver band meant to symbolize love and loyalty. And then I turn on the disposal and throw it in. Afterward, I reach inside, grab the warped ring, and toss it in the wastebasket. Why continue to wear the simple band that's meant to symbolize trust and loyalty when I'm the only one who kept my vows?

I wipe my hands with a paper towel and walk to the entrance of the family room, leaning against the doorframe to watch Stephen and Sunita. He's pointing to the island, a small piece of land with a few scattered trees and rocks, where the warblers and grebes perch and chatter. Sunita looks up at Stephen, still holding his hand, and I feel queasy when I think of how she was conceived. Was it against the wall, on the floor, in a bed? Did she taste better than me? You said it was only the one time. Do I believe you?

* * *

"Why didn't you tell me as soon as you came back?" I'd asked that night.

Stephen had hung his head. "I didn't want to hurt you."

"How noble of you. And this is *so* much better. For five years, you kept your affair…"

"It wasn't an affair," he interrupted. "It was *one* night."

"How do I really know that? Don't all men say it didn't mean anything. It was only once? How could you come home and pretend everything was the same?"

"There's more," he said.

"What? What more?"

"I just found out that Esha is dead, and I have a five-year-old daughter."

"Sweet Jesus," I said, holding my stomach like I'd been shot.

"The letter came this morning from an attorney representing an orphanage in Gujarat. My name is on the birth certificate."

"You didn't wear protection?"

Stephen sat there, shaking his head with his eyes closed.

"Oh. I see. It was one of those spontaneous moments when passion overcame the consequences. And the only reason you're telling me now is because there's a child? You son of a bitch."

And then I walked to the bathroom and puked. I left the house that night and ended up parked by the high school playground, staring at the tennis courts. Half of me wanted to go to a club, pick up a guy and screw his brains out. The other half wanted to run away. I didn't go home that night until the first school bus rolled into the parking lot the next morning.

* * *

I turn on the radio, hoping it will lighten my mood, but John Mayer is singing, *Daughters*, and I frown at the irony. I try to think of something, anything, that makes me happy right now. It used to be my job as manager of Village Books. Happy to once recommend new books and explain their premises, now I'm lethargic, pointing vaguely to a bookshelf. When asked to gift-wrap, I want to slide the book back and say, "Please wrap it yourself."

Last week, a young woman asked for Stephen's book, *Talk to a Terrorist*, and I wanted to whisper in her ear, "He's a great writer, but underneath, he's a lying cheat."

One night, when Paul Delaney, the owner, and I were closing up, he'd tried to kiss me.

"Let me get that for you," he said from behind while I was on the ladder. He'd put his hand on my back and helped me down. "Grace," he murmured in a husky voice, his lips brushing my cheek. I'd turned away, knowing it was wrong. But Stephen hadn't turned *his* head, had he? Maybe I should give Paul a call and tell him I am ready for a torrid affair and wild monkey sex. Then, I could tell Stephen and see how he reacts.

* * *

Stephen and Sunita come in the back door. She passes by and gives me a little smile. Can a five-year-old possibly sense what I am feeling?

"Yes, you can swim there," he's saying. "Do you swim, Sunita?"

"Yes. I was taught when I was young so I would not drown," she says in a lilting voice with perfect annunciation. She looks at me, and I wonder if she's looking for my approval.

I think of when she's a teenager, if she will lose her accent or use the word "wicked." Then again, I'm not sure I'll be here when Sunita is a teenager.

"Make sure she washes her hands before dinner," I say over my shoulder.

***

When Stephen came back from Gujarat, our lovemaking became mechanical. There was nothing clinically wrong with either of us, yet I still failed to conceive. We threw ourselves into projects like remodeling the house, creating an English garden, and designing a cobblestone patio and walkways so that we wouldn't focus solely on getting pregnant. We paid attention to everything but each other, and when we began to try again, the playfulness and lengthy foreplay were missing. We still said, "I love you," before hanging up the phone or going to sleep. In retrospect, had Stephen's adultery haunted him? Or had our lovemaking become too routine, lacking any real passion? We never talked about the change in our relationship, both of us accepting that over time all marriages change. Maybe not talking was our problem.

If he'd told me about Esha then, perhaps the shock of Sunita would have been less likely to devastate me now. He had hidden his secret so well—how many other secrets was he keeping from me?

Stephen had always refused to consider adoption or any other form of fertility treatment, holding out hope that I would get pregnant eventually. The last time I brought up the subject, he said, "Grace. I come from a family of five kids, for Christ's sake. Mark was born when my mother was forty-six. You're thirty-seven; there's still plenty of time."

Little did he know he'd already fathered a child.

At the table, Stephen and Sunita continue their dialogue while I fiddle with my food. "This is delicious," says Stephen. I can't remember the last time Stephen complimented my cooking, and it feels insincere. But Sunita nods, agreeing with Stephen's comment.

"Thanks," I say. He's put a pillow under Sunita because she's too small for the table. She has good manners, placing the napkin on her lap and making a concerted effort to close her mouth while she chews.

"Sunita told me she's going to be in the first grade," Stephen says.

"That's nice," I say. There's a long, uncomfortable silence as silverware scrapes against plates. Sunita starts to fall off the pillow, and I watch as Stephen gently lifts her small body and repositions her.

"I'll clear the table. Why don't you two sit in the living room, and I'll join you later," I say.

I linger alone in the kitchen and rinse off the dishes slowly while I weigh the consequences of leaving Stephen. I'd started reading some of the self-help books in the store, like *Why Do Men Cheat?* and *Pissed Off*, looking for answers. I finish wiping down the counters and turn the night light on over the kitchen stove. As I walk into the living room, I hear Stephen's voice. He has the large picture book of Switzerland propped on his lap.

"That's the Shilthorn. Beautiful, isn't it?"

"Can you climb it?" Sunita asks.

"Absolutely," he says and looks at me.

I remember that vacation in Switzerland. How afraid I am of heights, but did it anyway, because I knew how much he wanted to go to the top. The further we went up on the gondola, the more afraid I became. Stephen put his arms around me and said, "I'm right here, Grace. It's okay. Close your eyes; you're doing great." I buried my head in his chest and felt intensely protected, that nothing bad would ever happen to me as long as Stephen was there.

* * *

I sit down in the chair by the window and pick up *The New Yorker*. Every so often, I glance at Sunita and Stephen when I think they're not looking. I know Stephen wants us to stay together, for me to be part of Sunita's life. All he asks for right now is forgiveness. And all I want is to make everything go away.

I think of the woman being paged at the airport this morning. How I'd imagined myself being paged. "Grace Moore, please come to the information desk in Terminal E. Grace Moore, please pick up your new life, then you are free to move on."

I sigh, exhausted from the stress of the past few weeks but afraid of the dreams and the tossing and turning that bed will bring. Stephen looks up, and I stare straight at him for the first time in weeks. Sunita looks at Stephen and then at me, and I see the question in her eyes. *What's going on with you two?* It's easy to see she's a sensitive child with the same contemplative looks as her father.

"I'll be right back," he announces, walking toward the bathroom.

I wish Stephen had the face of a camel and that he was mean-spirited so that it would be easier to hate him. But he has the body of a basketball player, tall and muscular. His long, dark blonde hair is combed back from his face, and he has blue, deep-set eyes that reflect his thoughtful moods. He's wearing a wrinkled white shirt, jeans, and running shoes. He's a good man, the kind you want around when there's a problem, a take-charge kind of guy with confidence and no arrogance. No wonder Esha fell for him.

Sunita and I are alone for the first time since the airport ladies' room and I remember the butterfly necklace.

"I have something for you," I say, reaching for my handbag beside the chair. I walk over to Sunita and hand her the small box.

"Thank you," she says.

"You're welcome."

Sunita opens the box and looks at the tiny necklace with the butterfly charm. "*Papillon,*" she says with a perfect accent.

"Yes. Do you speak French?" I ask.

"No. I only know *papillon* means butterfly because Mother spoke French. She showed me a butterfly in the garden one day. She called it *papillon* so I did also."

Ah yes, Esha, Stephen's lover, who spoke French and English and Gujarati and was probably gorgeous. She, with the caramel skin and silky black hair, who gave him the child I never could. Sunita yawns and covers her mouth politely. Stephen comes out of the bathroom.

"I think she might like to get ready for bed," I tell him. "It's been a long day."

"Of course. I can help her." He turns to Sunita. "Do you have pajamas with you?"

"Yes."

"What is that?" he asks, looking at the box she's holding in her hand.

Sunita looks at me proudly and says, "*Papillon.*" I feel a tiny spark of pride that she likes my gift.

Stephen becomes overly enthusiastic. "You bought that?"

"It's nothing, Stephen, just a piece of little girl jewelry."

But I can tell it means more to Stephen. I watch them go upstairs, wondering why Sunita is so at ease with him. Had Esha told her about her father? That he's a good man and has an important job, and lives far away? Did she mention he had a wife?

Sunita says, "Good night, Grace. Thank you for my necklace."

I'm pleased by her thoughtfulness.

"Good night, Sunita. Sleep well."

She gives me a half smile and follows Stephen.

A few minutes later, he comes to the top of the stairs. "Grace, I'm going to read Sunita, *The Snow Queen,* and make sure she's tucked in. I won't be long."

"Fine," I say, searching for the copy of *Pissed Off.*

* * *

The next morning, I throw up and Sunita pees the bed. I am in the kitchen making tea when Stephen passes me on the way to the laundry room, the soiled sheets in his arms. He looks at me, frowning and embarrassed. I put a slice of bread in the toaster.

Every night for two weeks, Sunita wets the bed. I'm assuming it's the adjustment to her surroundings and that stress comes out in different ways for everyone. We control her fluids beforehand, and Stephen wakes her every morning at two o'clock to take her to the bathroom. The bedwetting starts to slow down, and Stephen rewards Sunita with a trip to the homemade ice cream stand. I remain a background figure, struggling with angst and a broken heart. I go to work, run every day, and try to keep up with the gardening, but my mind wanders. I picture Stephen and Esha in bed, having dinner and laughing together.

He takes a leave of absence from work and enrolls Sunita in a preschool program before she starts first grade in September. He brings her to the pediatrician and buys her new clothes. She likes pink and buys her Disney princess dolls, a bedspread and sheets, and framed pictures of Ariel, Belle, and Mulan. He teaches her to bounce a basketball and installs a smaller version of his own hoop so she can learn to shoot.

There are moments when I look at Sunita and sense a stirring, a feeling I cannot articulate. Whenever she catches my eye, she touches the necklace and smiles. I know it's her way of showing appreciation. She's a sweet girl, and I can tell she is trying hard to not be a bother.

Normally, she waits for me to make the first move toward communication, yet she is always compliant when I tell her to get ready for bed or when I French-braid her hair. She likes that and runs her hand along the back of her head. One day, when I lifted my arm to tuck in a stray hair, Sunita saw the tattoo I'd been hiding, pointing to my thigh.

"What is that?" she asked.

"It's a seahorse, but don't tell anyone," I said, putting my finger to my lips. Sunita nodded and covered her mouth, giggling. Stephen hated tattoos, so the week after he told me about Esha and Sunita, I'd driven down to Provincetown and had it done. I'd drawn the small green and blue seahorse myself for the tattooist to copy. I picked the seahorse for its colors—and because it is the only male species that gets pregnant and gives birth.

Every night, Stephen tells me he loves me, but I don't answer. I am neither rude nor affectionate toward him. He tells me he knows it will take time. But I'm not convinced time is the answer.

* * *

When the nausea increases, I visit my doctor. The thought of being pregnant flits through my mind, but because of my history of nausea and lack of success getting pregnant, I dismiss the idea. I am more tired than I've ever been and wonder if I'm anemic or perhaps have an ulcer.

But Dr. Hopkins tells me I'm going to have a baby, and I am stunned.

I realize then that I've completely lost track of my periods. I am nine weeks pregnant, and the doctor says that my child is already forming its toes. I try to pay attention to what the doctor is saying, but I keep thinking about Stephen's reaction.

"...and continue work, gardening, and running. I'll see you in a few weeks for a checkup. Congratulations, Grace. I'm very happy for Stephen and you."

When I get home Stephen and Sunita are out. I run upstairs and take my clothes off in front of the mirror. My breasts seem a bit fuller, and the areolas seem a bit darker. But my abdomen is still flat. When I turn to the side, I imagine how it will look in a few months and then at full term. I close my eyes and hug myself, overjoyed by this blessing. As petty as it seems, I feel I am now on equal ground with Esha.

I do not tell Stephen that I'm pregnant for nearly two weeks. I want to hold on to my secret for a while longer, just me and my tiny baby, who already has its toes. Will it be a girl or a boy? Do I want to know? And what will its name be? I've always loved the name Stephanie for a girl and Jake for a boy.

* * *

Tonight, Sunita takes her plate and glass to the kitchen counter.

"Thank you, honey," I say without thinking. Sunita looks up, and happiness is spread all over her face. She's proud because she hasn't wet the bed for four nights in a row. Filled with unexpected warmth, I lean over and hug her, feeling the bony little shoulders against my stomach. Sunita squeezes me around the waist, her head against my belly, then releases me, laughing. And I laugh with her. She hears Stephen in the driveway bouncing the basketball. "Are you going to shoot hoops with—Daddy?"

Sunita nods and runs out the back door as my eyes follow her. I think about the baby growing inside me—Sunita's half-sibling. For the past few weeks, I have looked back on my own troubled childhood and how I want things to be different for my own child.

* * *

My mother left for parts unknown when I was three, and I never saw her again. Living without a mother was tough, and I was shifted from one babysitter to another while my father worked. I never knew where I would stay next. I searched for my mother in the faces of other women throughout my life. There were no photos of her in the house, so I looked in the mirror constantly, wondering if we looked alike and if I would recognize her if I saw her on the street. I asked myself, *why did you leave? Why didn't you want me?* It was hard for my father to raise me alone, but I always knew he tried to be a good parent, working hard to put me through college.

As I thought more about my upbringing, I realized that if something were to happen to me, I would want someone to mother my child. I want Sunita to grow up with both parents, as I do my own, in a stable home like I had craved.

* * *

I ask myself now if Stephen would cheat on me again. Would he ever walk out on our family? Do I believe he loves me and made a horrible mistake? And do I have it in my heart to forgive him and raise our children together? And then I burst out crying, heaving sobs of heartache and happiness pouring out of me.

* * *

After a long while, I clean up the kitchen then walk outside to the back deck and sit down. I gaze at the colors of the setting sun; wondrous shades of gold, orange, and pink light up the horizon. The magic hour, I think as I watch dusk approach. The French call it *L'heure entre chien et loup*—the hour between dog and wolf.

Tonight's sunset seems particularly vibrant. I look up at the pines, whose branches are so high and close together they barely leave room for the sky. They are soothing as they weave gently in the nighttime breeze, and I can hear their boughs bend and creak. They have endured hurricanes, Nor'easters, and snow so heavy their thick branches look like amputations, yet still they keep growing and remain strong and beautiful. The whole area smells of bark and soil, lush with flowering rhododendrons in pink and lavender. I hear the birds, always chatty at this time of day, another part of nature we must preserve. Birdfeeders dangle from branches throughout the property so there's a constant stream of flying visitors on our land. This is the home I've created over the years with Stephen. The home I still love and where I want to remain.

I watch as a bird flutters down and lands on the rim of the birdbath in the center of the back yard. Behind it, the path leads to the lake and the sunset beyond. It's a vision that can't be replicated in the frame of a lens, but one that will stay in my mind longer than a photo in the drawer of a desk. A second bird lands, and then another, smaller and darker. I watch as they peck at the water, raise their heads, look quickly from right to left, and put their heads down again.

When a fourth bird lands, even smaller than the last one, I stand up and go to the railing. I watch the family of four birds for a long time, a feeling of hope and absolution filling my soul.

And then I walk back into the house to tell Stephen we are going to have another child.

Valhalla

Jay Cauley stands in his briefs in front of the bathroom mirror with a colander on his head. He's wedged a spray of seagull feathers in each handle and imagines himself jumping off a Viking long ship. Leaning closer to the mirror, he strokes his jaw, estimating it will be another few days before his beard is in full warrior mode. Yesterday, he shaved both sides of his head, leaving only a tuft of brown hair at the top, now covered by his new helmet.

For nearly two weeks, in a basement apartment of an old converted mansion, Jay's been buried under snow due to the worst Nor'easter in years. He is the only one in the massive house, and the winds are howling and creepy, like a pack of wolves running around in circles. The neighbors in the first-floor condo left for St. John in November, the people on the second floor moved out, and before the blizzard, the third floor was being renovated. The remaining estates fronting West Beach are used only as summer homes.

He checks his right ear, where a large paperclip dangles from the piercing he did two days ago with a sewing needle. Though it's only ten o'clock in the morning, he takes a swig from a small glass of Jameson's and sets it on the back of the toilet. "Loneliness does strange things to a man," he tells Magnus, his Maine Coon cat, who sits on the toilet seat watching.

A data analyst at a large biotech company in Boston, Jay's been working from home since the pandemic. But the power went out the day of the storm, and he hasn't had access to the Internet since. He's afraid that if his solitude lasts much longer—he'll go nuts.

Every day, the walls are closing in little by little. Jay used to love his apartment, but now he feels like he's been kidnapped and thrown into a cold, dark dungeon. The kerosene lamp reminds him of the oil lamps used in medieval times, and he thinks of what people did inside their huts of stone and mud floors. Animal charades? Pin the tail on the wild boar?

He studies the image he's trying to create and wishes he had some bright blue paint so he could draw a Celtic cross on his forehead. Then he remembers the sheepskin jacket he's had for years. He runs to the bedroom and finds it in the back of the closet. Cutting the sleeves off, he makes it into a vest and slips it on. Pants are a problem, but his sister, Kathleen, left a pair of black yoga pants on her last visit, so he tried those on. The pants are snug, but they work. Jay is not a big man. In fact, he's only five feet six, the guy who's always sitting or kneeling in the first row of group photos.

Next, he finds his Tevas and adds a pair of wool socks to the sandals. Back in the bathroom, he checks himself out again. Standing up straight, he adjusts his vest and says, "Now we're getting somewhere! Why didn't I come up with this getup when it counted?" he asks the cat. "Maybe if I'd shown more creativity, she might've gone out with me again."

Magnus looks down at his paws.

"Wasn't gonna happen, was it?"

Magnus looks away.

* * *

Riva Matthews is a woman he'd met at the Union Oyster House Bar in Boston in early December. Initially, he thought she was way out of his league, stunning and sophisticated. The best part was that she was only a little taller than him. They'd hit it off immediately when she knocked over his drink with her pocketbook on the way to the lady's room.

"Whoa!" he said. "You could've just asked my name if you wanted to meet me."

She'd laughed and bought the next two rounds. They talked until the place closed, then sat outside on a park bench warmed by alcohol, laughing and telling silly jokes. Riva was a personal shopper for some pretty wealthy clients and had a lot of funny stories to tell—without names, of course. It was a magical night for Jay as a light snow drifted around them. He'd never fallen so fast for anyone as he had for her. In his late thirties, he'd actually given up on finding the right one. He'd had the occasional crushes and short-term relationships, the one-night stands, but this was something different. He knew he was a goner, and if she'd asked him to jump off the Zakim Bridge, he would have done it in a second.

A day later, when he got her text inviting him to a New Year's Eve masquerade party, he was like a teenager on his first date. But she neglected to tell him it was at the Park Plaza Hotel.

Riva showed up as Audrey Hepburn in *Breakfast at Tiffany's:* big black sunglasses, long cigarette holder, black dress and pearls, and her long, dark hair piled on top of her head. He was dazzled by her elegance and couldn't stop staring. Unfortunately, Jay had worn a Red Sox jacket and baseball cap and told her he was dressed as a Red Sox fan.

She never made fun of him, never told him she was disappointed or that it wasn't good enough. She simply said, "I see. Well, come on then, slugger."

When they got to the hotel, he was mortified by his lack of imagination. The large ballroom was like a circus. The first thing he saw was a woman in a ballet costume, pedaling a stuffed animal horse that whinnied. Another woman was dressed as a Geisha girl flying a Japanese kite activated by a large fan. The winner was Robinson Crusoe, who was bare-chested, carried an umbrella, wore a goatskin hat, and a pair of breeches. The tour de force was an actual talking parrot perched on his shoulder.

Jay felt like Riva's kid brother following her around the room. He could tell her friends thought he was a loser, the way they were checking him out. When they left the party, she'd called an Uber rather than driving home with him. Jay hadn't even bothered to call her. Then again, she hadn't called or texted him either. The thing is, he still thinks about her all the time. She is, as they say, "the one who got away," the one who still lives in his dreams—her face like a beautiful apparition that never faded from his mind.

"What do you think, Magnus? Maybe I should take a selfie and send it to her."

Magnus squints in response.

Jay reaches out to pet him, but Magnus jumps off the toilet. "It's the helmet, isn't it? You don't like the helmet."

He wishes Riva were here so they could cuddle and keep each other company. Maybe he should have called her. Maybe they could have laughed it off. Maybe she would've been happy to hear from him again. But his own insecurity had stopped him. Maybe, maybe, maybe… Jay covers his face with his hands, silently scolding himself for overthinking everything lately. He's well aware it's important to keep busy so he won't go crazy, but there's a good chance he's already crazy, and this is what it feels like.

He looks around his spacious apartment with its low-ceilinged beams. It has one large bedroom, a decent-sized bathroom, and an island that divides the kitchen from the living room, where there's a small wood fireplace. Two walls of floor-to-ceiling bookcases hold a variety of novels such as *All the Light We Cannot See, Atonement, Disappearing Earth, Lion of Ireland,* and *Under Occupation,* which he filed alphabetically last week. His movie collection is comprised of *Braveheart, Gladiator, Troy,* the complete series of *Homeland, The Mists of Avalon,* and *Wedding Crashers*—also in alphabetical order. His music varies from classical to jazz to contemporary artists like Ed Sheeran and Billie Eilish. But his favorites are movie soundtracks like *The Mask of Zorro* and *The Last of the Mohicans,* when he closes his eyes, and pictures specific scenes that match the score.

Jay looks up at the ceiling and around the room, trying to figure out what will keep him occupied until his next nap. And then he spots the Sharpie on the coffee table.

Grabbing the black pen, he sits on the couch, removes his Tevas and socks, and rolls up his sister's pants. Carefully, he tries to reproduce a snake winding its way between each toe and crawling up his leg. He draws a head with a black eye and a darting tongue. After it dries, he puts his socks and sandals back on and sits back, lifting the colander and scratching the side of his head where he shaved.

Earlier, he'd cleaned out his medicine cabinet, leaving only a bottle of aspirin, a tube of toothpaste, and a stick of deodorant. His bureau drawers are divided by color, and the kitchen cabinets have all the cans and bottles facing outward. He's re-arranged his bedroom several times, finished the 1,000-word puzzle of Julius Caesar's Roman Empire, and made a list of every single person he can remember from high school for no reason except to keep busy. He's thinking about shaving off his eyebrows later today just to see how it looks.

To keep his quarters as dry and warm as possible, he's had to stand on a stepladder to stuff the sills of the high basement windows with old newspapers and towels. His front door and the steps up and out to the beach are barricaded by snow. He is down to his last few candles but still has plenty of kerosene for the lamp. Last night, he lit his last fire and is now completely out of wood. One battery is left in his flashlight, and he's slowly running out of food. The whiskey keeps him warm when he's not doing pushups, and the sheepskin vest is helping.

Before the blizzard, he'd bought five bottles of Jameson's and is now down to one. Three months into the pandemic, he ran out of weed, and no one else had any left either.

As he lay in bed the night before, he actually thought he had the virus. His head hurt; he had a sore throat and dry cough and immediately panicked. With no thermometer in the house, he couldn't tell if he had a fever. He imagined himself dying alone, slowly, unable to breathe. Just thinking about it made his heart beat faster. But this morning, except for being cold, he felt okay.

He pours himself another glass of the golden nectar of the Gods and takes three gulps.

"I shall fight this pandemic with strength and honor!" he yells to Magnus, who puts his paw over his eyes.

Suddenly, Jay runs into the living room, jumps on the hassock, and yells, "KILL THE ENGLISH!" He raises his fist to the sky like Mel Gibson in *Braveheart*. Magnus vaults from the floor to the windowsill. He stares down at Jay as if Jay is a madman.

"*Sláinte Mhaith,*" he yells, the Gaelic words for good health. From the hassock, he jumps to the coffee table and sees the poker beside the fireplace.

"Aha!" he hollers, leaping off the table and retrieving the tool. Running to the back hall, he finds a cardboard box, flattens it and cuts out a triangle. He covers it in tinfoil like a shield, and around his waist, he belts a green tie to hold it in place. Then he rushes to the center of the apartment the poker hanging by his side. Turning around in slow motion, he hollers, "ARE YOU ENTERTAINED?" like Russell Crowe in *Gladiator*. He finishes his whiskey and throws the glass against the wall, where it shatters. For a few moments, he feels strong and invincible.

After trotting back and forth through the apartment as if he's riding a horse with pretend reins, he lifts his leg in a semicircle as if he's dismounting. He then stabs his poker several times in the air, dueling like a master of the sword.

Out of breath and hungry, he finds the last piece of bread in the loaf, a nice thick heel, and spreads honey on it, savoring each bite and wondering how long he can last. Thankfully, he still has running water. Then, he cleans up the broken glass with a dustpan and brush.

* * *

His friend, Yin-Shan, lives in Boston on the sixth floor of an apartment complex. Jay is jealous because he has plenty of natural light during the day. But neither of them has been in contact since the power went out and stopped using their cells except for an emergency. He misses their Thursday night chess games, and dinner and drinks in Chinatown. Jay's sister, Kathleen, called to check on him before the blizzard, but he hasn't talked to her since. He thinks about Riva and hopes she's okay. In the back of his mind, he is saving at least one bar on his cell, in case he sums up enough courage to call or text her. Has she put him on her "Never, ever" list? Does he even rate a place on her list? He thinks not.

Jay opens the last bottle of Jameson's and takes a few swigs. He sits on the couch and stares into the fireplace, looking at last night's ashes. Squinting, he thinks he sees something move. He walks over and bends down to look closer, wondering if a mouse got in there. His colander starts to tip and he holds it in place as he waits and watches. Then, he sees a small tail wiggling under the cinders. He jumps back, and his helmet falls on the floor while his heart does a somersault. For a long time, he sits on the couch until his eyes start to swim, and eventually, he nods off.

Twenty minutes later, Jay wakes up with a start when he hears screeching and clawing in the wall behind him. More mice? What if hundreds of them are crawling through the walls and coming down the fireplace to form an army? He stands and walks behind the couch, putting his ear against the wall. He cups his hands and hisses, "I know you're in there, but I have kerosene, and I will burn you out." It seems to stop, and Jay relaxes a bit. But when he walks away, he hears it again. And then he pummels the wall and screams, "Go away, you little shits!"

But he backs away, terrified when he swears it says, "You go away, Jay…"

Disoriented and feeling completely helpless, Jay starts to cry. What is happening to him? He hasn't cried since his Siberian Husky, Loki, died four years ago. Why are there all these mice in his apartment all of a sudden? He looks to the fireplace again and thinks he sees more than one tail now, but if he opens the glass door—they'll all come out and run around the apartment. He backs up to the couch and automatically pulls his feet up. But the mice continue making noise, so he runs to his bedroom, jumps into bed, and pulls the covers over his head.

He dreams of Riva, in a *Pirates of the Caribbean* outfit, coming to save him from starvation and boredom.

"I think you still have potential," she says, standing over him in tall boots, a sword dangling from her belt. And then he wakes up abruptly when he hears his cell phone ring. But when he picks it up, there is no message, and there is no missed call.

His head feels thick and heavy, and he tilts as he slowly rises from the bed. His mouth is dry, and the ringing of his cell phone confuses him. He is not sure if he dreamed it or if he is still dreaming. He goes to the wall and listens. But the mice must have left. He looks in the fireplace and wonders where they've all gone. Have they found a pipe and crept up to the first-floor condo? Or are they regrouping?

In the kitchen, he gets a drink of water and once more hears his cell phone ring. He runs into the bedroom, tripping on the scatter rug, but the ringing stops before he gets there. Once again, there is no missed call. He looks at the bars and sees he has one left. But didn't he have two when he'd stopped using his phone? How could the other bar simply disappear? Now he's pissed. His brain is jumbled, and he wants to lash out and vent his anger and frustration.

Leaning against the island of his kitchen and trying to calm down, the next thing he hears is scraping outside his front door. He pauses as his heart starts to pound. It's all too much. He puts his hands over his ears, but the scraping continues. Out of sorts, he wobbles to the door, where his surfboard leans against the wall. Jay is no scaredy cat. He took boxing in college and has been in plenty of fights as a kid growing up in Charlestown. Although the other kids were bigger, Jay was quicker. He's never thrown the first punch, but he's usually still standing at the end. But the battle is different now because Jay doesn't realize that the real opponent is Jay himself.

The scraping continues, and he stands at the door, holding his head and rocking frontward and backward. He thinks of what the inside of his head looks like and envisions dried seaweed, dark and wiry with tangles of tiny black knots and patchy sand. It is clogging his thought process, his memory, and his ability to reason.

As he watches in horror, the doorknob slowly turns. Did he not lock it the last time he went out before the storm?

"Magnus," he whispers, "There is fuckery amongst us!"

Magnus runs to the bedroom and disappears under the bed.

Jay goes into the living room, picks up the fire poker, and puts his helmet back on. Sweat runs down his face and chest. He takes a deep breath, summoning the courage of his movie heroes. His adrenaline starts to pump and then skyrockets as if he's been waiting for this attack all along.

When a brown-gloved hand cups the frame of the door, trying to push it in, Jay raises the poker high over his head. The light from outside temporarily impairs his vision, and all he can see is the outline of a man with a black beanie like looters wear, trying to get through the door.

"Ahhh!" Jay yells in his best battle cry. He feels the rage within him overtake his mind and body with no conscious thought of what he is about to do. When the man is almost through the door, Jay smashes him over the head again and again with the poker as hard as he can. The man falls to the floor and lies still. Jay is panting so hard he can't catch his breath. He feels a sudden pain shoot through his chest.

When it stops, he flips the body over and realizes it's the property manager, Tom Hanscomb, not an intruder or burglar trying to break in. He bends down and feels for a pulse, but there is none. Tom's eyes are wide open, staring at the ceiling, as blood seeps from his head like a red puddle on the floor.

"Oh God—Oh no!" Jay cries. He starts shaking so badly that he drops the poker. He is sickened by what he has done and slowly sinks to the floor, bawling like a newborn.

"I'm so sorry, Tom!" he wails. "What in hell have I done to you?"

Tom is not just the property manager. He is Jay's friend, a veteran surfer who taught Jay everything he knows about surfing; he went with him to buy his first wetsuit and taught him how to bottom turn, foam climb, and cutback. Until he met Riva, they were the best times of his life.

After a long time and exhausted from crying, Jay gets up and opens the door all the way. The storm is over, and the light outside is turning. Jay sees that Tom has scraped the stairs with a shovel down to the apartment to get to him. To save him.

In a Viking mindset, Jay believes Tom is a hero, a true soldier of war who had tried to come to his aid. He knows now what he must do. He must give his hero a proper Viking burial.

Jay finds a white sheet in the linen closet and wraps Tom's body tightly, leaving his head uncovered. He puts him in his sleeping bag and drags him out the door and up the steps, where he lays him on the snow. Back down in the apartment, he lifts his surfboard and brings it back up where he gently places Tom's body with his shovel on top, evidence of his bravery. He ties the body and the shovel to the board with ropes. Lastly, Jay closes Tom's eyes and places a large strainer on his face to protect him on his way to the afterlife.

When the sun begins to descend, and the sky is streaked in magnificent hues of orange, pink, and purple, Jay drags the surfboard over the dune and down to the ocean, tripping twice in his Tevas but holding tight to the burial board. Not a soul is in sight. Trying to stay focused, he drags the board across the sand and walks knee-deep into the water. He is shaking so badly that he can hardly pour the kerosene over Tom's body. Next, he tosses in several lit wooden matches and pushes the board as far as he can into the water with what little energy he has left. He is gasping for air as he watches the polyurethane chemicals catch. A giant fire lights up the ocean, creating a proper Viking bonfire. Jay gazes in awe at the sight and, in his crazed mind, he has done the honorable thing.

He hauls himself out of the water, unable to stop trembling. He staggers toward home, falling in the snow many times on his way. Finally, as he climbs to the top of the dune, he looks back at the burning board and the darkening sky, where a few stars are just beginning to appear. He watches as a giant eagle soars over the setting sun, and he bows his head in homage. Tom is passing through the clouds on his way to Valhalla.

Soaked and numb, Jay shivers violently as he makes his way down the dune only steps away from his apartment. He can hear his phone ring and believes now that it is Riva calling. His heart squeezes at the thought—but the squeezing turns to a sharp pain in the center of his chest, much worse than the last one. He sinks to his knees, and starts to dry heave. The pain spreads across the trunk of his body to his arms, and the phone keeps ringing, and ringing, and ringing until it fades into nothingness. Jay knows he's not going to get there in time, as he feels himself slipping—from this world to the next.

Expiration Date

Rocco's, the local hangout for Mass General Hospital employees, buzzed with the name Red Costello, the powerful Irish mafia king shot that afternoon on the tarmac at Logan Airport while trying to escape imprisonment. Arrested after sixteen years on the lam, Costello was accused of nineteen murders, racketeering, and firearms possession. He was now lying in a bed at Mass General under heavy guard.

Inside the restaurant, the pungent smell of garlic, frying meatballs, oregano, and tomato sauce filled the air while Sinatra crooned *Come Fly with Me*. Lining the walls were photos of a younger Rocco shaking hands with Carl Yastrzemski, Bobby Orr, Teddy Kennedy, Matt Damon, and Ben Affleck.

It was Thursday night, and Sarah and I were sitting in our usual booth in the corner by the window, sharing a bottle of Rioja. We'd first met fifteen years ago at orientation as new employees of the hospital.

Sarah was a bit quirky, but when it came to writing code or developing a website, she was a rock star. Today's get-up featured a large half-moon and star necklace, long yellow feather earrings, and a plunging 1960s psychedelic flower top. Her blonde hair was in some kind of updo with jeweled bobby pins. I couldn't decide if she looked like a fortune teller or if she'd joined an alternate reality group.

"We haven't had this much pandemonium since the marathon bombings," I said, pushing my heels off under the table and wiggling my toes like finger puppets. I hate heels, but they make me look important at meetings.

"I know, the cops were swarming the White Lobby."

I took a deep breath, signaling my boredom with life. "How was your week?" I asked.

"I have a low red cell count."

"Okay," I said, in my patient advocate voice. "It's probably a B-12 deficiency."

"What if it's not? What if it's leukemia?"

Being employed at a hospital meant we were all hypochondriacs, diagnosing every symptom as a worst-case scenario. A headache might mean a brain tumor. Nausea – most likely stomach cancer. And if you were over tired, lupus or leukemia immediately came to mind.

"I like the way the Druids buried their dead," she said out of nowhere. "They believed in reincarnation, which I seriously believe in, or I'd never be able to deal with death."

"So now you're a Druid?"

"I'm just saying," she said, leaning her head left as a feather earring swung out. "They believed in the otherworld and that when we die, the soul is continually reborn until we fully acquire wisdom and love."

"Sarah. You have a low red cell count. It doesn't mean you're dying."

"But what if it *is* something serious? Isn't it better to believe there's life after death so we're not so afraid of it? Besides that, I'm getting closer to my expiration date."

"You're not even forty yet."

"Close enough. I'm almost halfway to eighty, and eighty-one point six is the average life span for a woman."

"Hmm." I took a healthy gulp of wine. "When will you know the results?"

"Not sure," she said, leaning her arms on the table, her voluminous freckled chest resembling paprika on an uncooked chicken. "And I haven't been feeling well lately. I'm tired a lot."

"So's the rest of the world. Look. Until you get those test results, don't be planning your funeral."

"You know the Druids also dressed the body in ceremonial clothing and buried it with keepsakes so the spirit could carry on in the next life."

"Really," I say, trying not to yawn.

"I'm thinking of a book. Maybe *Proof of Heaven* and fir tree branches tucked into the sides of the coffin."

I gave her a weird look.

"What? The Druids *loved* nature."

"I see."

Just then, an ambulance rounded the corner, red lights flashing and sirens blasting as cars pulled over. Sarah watched as it drove up to the emergency entrance of the hospital.

"Okay, Marie," she said, pointing to the ambulance.

"What if that person ran six miles last night? What if he or she refused that chocolate chip cookie or nice warm brownie with hazelnut ice cream on top after dinner? Now they're probably going to die of a heart attack." Sarah slapped her hand on the table, and I jerked backward.

"What good did it do? All this worry about being in shape is really about being afraid of dying. We're all going to the big white tent in the sky someday. Why not embrace it?"

Sarah finished her wine and poured herself another glass. "And the reason I don't want to be cremated? Because the flames burn right through the box, so the casket and my remains are in one urn, and when they toss my ashes into the sea? It'll be part me and part plantation teak floating in the whitecaps."

"I see you've given this a lot of thought."

I looked over her shoulder and barely moved my mouth like a ventriloquist.

"Warning —Vida the Valley Girl is coming over."

"*Super,*" Sarah said with a lisp.

"Hey dudettes," said Vida. "Awesome blouse, Marie. Brings out those blue eyes to the max!" Vida is a curly redhead in her mid-thirties, and acted like she was seventeen. But she has an MBA, and Mass General likes that.

"Thanks," I responded with the enthusiasm of floating seaweed.

"How are you, Vida?" asked Sarah.

Vida bent down like she was about to reveal the code names of the top KGB operatives.

"I'm like totally drowning in all this bogus paperwork. As if? The money's super good, but it's, like, way too much for one person. I'm like a total mess.

OMG, look at me."

"You look the same to me," I said.

Vida put her beer bottle on the table and pulled both eyelids down. "Look! They're, like, almost white!"

Sarah and I peered at Vida, who looked like a kid trying to scare her mother.

"I'm anemic for sure," she said, nodding her head. She took a swig from her beer and sighed. "What*evah*."

Sarah tried not to laugh when I crossed my eyes.

"Vida," Sarah said, clearing her throat. "I don't mean to hurt your feelings, but I need some heart-to-heart here with Marie."

"Totally. No prob. See you on Ether Day!"

* * *

Leaning back, Sarah pulled her left bra strap up and said, "Know what I read recently?"

I tucked my hair behind my ear. "*The Five People You Meet in Heaven?*

"Good guess—but no. According to Dr. Sherwin Nuland, God rest his soul, he wrote *How We Die: Reflections on Life's Final Chapter.* The upshot of one of his theories is that when the body is under extreme stress, it gives off these chemicals that put it in some sort of trance. My interpretation of this is that when someone murders you, maybe you don't feel the stabbing or the gunshot for all that long. Or, if your plane blows up, you don't die immediately, but lay there without pain, staring up at your future home."

My eyes widened.

"You know those rays that sometimes come straight down from the sky on a clear day?"

I nodded, wondering what was coming.

"Well, that's when your body takes the magic elevator straight to the afterlife," she said, slanting her hand up in the air like we were going there any minute.

"Really."

Moving in closer, she whispered in a low voice, "Of course, it's an invisible parade of bodies because only a few of us recognize the significance of what's really happening."

I'd just taken a large sip of wine when it spurted from my mouth like a garden hose.

"You, okay?" asked Sarah.

I wiped my mouth with a napkin and signaled the waitress.

"Where the hell do you get this stuff?"

"I read a lot."

Gina, our waitress, approached and said, "Gonna tie one on tonight girls?" Sponging the wine off the table and laughing, she added, "I can always book you a room at the Wyndham." With a new bottle of wine nestled against her stomach, she popped the cork.

"I'll bring some bread to help sop up the booze," she said and walked away.

"Okay. Enough about me. What's going on with you?"

"Nothing. Ab-so-lute-ly nothing," I said. "My life is so friggin' boring it's ridiculous. Want to know the highlights of my week?"

She nodded emphatically, earrings bouncing like ponytails.

"Okay. Rocco's with you on Thursday nights and *Law & Order* reruns. Jealous?"

"Oh honey, I'm sorry. What about knitting?"

I squinted to see if she was kidding. But she was dead serious.

"I'll be thirty-five next week, and by now, I should be married, have a few kids sitting around a table, and a cute little house with a window nook. Or, at the very least, be in a flaming, red-hot relationship." I paused. "Remember that song, 'Is That All There Is?' by Peggy Lee?"

"I do."

"That's me."

Sarah studied me closely. "Maybe you're still hung up on that guy from Ireland."

"That was thirteen years ago. Who knows what's happened to him."

"But you do mention him a lot, Marie. Ever think about getting in touch?"

"Sometimes. But he's probably forgotten who I am."

"Oh, I doubt it. You're so beautiful with all that black hair and gorgeous smile. Who could forget you, sweetie?"

Maybe it was the wine or Frank Sinatra segueing into "I've Got You Under My Skin", but Sarah noticed and gave me a sad look, which was all I needed as my eyes watered.

Just as we clinked glasses, we heard the loud screeching of tires closing in on the restaurant. Both of us looked out the window at the same time.

"That ambulance is coming down the street way too fast, don't you think?" said Sarah.

"Hell, yes."

Then, instead of taking a sharp left onto Cambridge Street from Mass General's main entrance, the ambulance lost control and headed straight for Rocco's.

"Holy shit! Get under the table!" I yelled, scooting below. But Sarah struggled, trying to squeeze the top half of her body underneath.

"Pull my legs!" she shouted.

I yanked as Sarah flattened her breasts with both hands, pushing her butt off the seat. But she only lowered the bottom half of her body.

Within seconds, a deafening blast shook the building as the ambulance crashed through the front of Rocco's, forty feet from where we were sitting. The restaurant exploded into shattering glass and falling beams—the floors and walls vibrating with the impact, creating a blizzard of dust and drywall.

The ambulance stopped perpendicular to the bar, its horn blaring like a cruise ship before departure. From under the table, all I saw was Sarah's lower half and the triangle of her leopard undies. "Sarah!" I screamed, "Are you alright?"

"Yeah. You?"

"Yes."

"Can you see anything?" she asked, trying to turn around.

I peeked out from under the table.

"Looks like a guy in a stretcher with red hair, a man slumped over the horn, and another guy in the passenger seat leaning against the window."

The restaurant looked like a bombsite, and people were coughing and moaning. And then I watched as the passenger door to the van opened. The horn stopped, and a tall, muscular man with thick black hair got out and slammed the door. His eyes darted around the room like a ferret, and he pulled out a gun from his back waistband, letting it hang at his side.

In a thick accent, he said, "Everyone stay calm 'n keep yer traps shut."

The room became silent except for the muffled sounds of hacking. My breath caught in my throat, and my mouth dropped.

"What do you want?" Rocco hollered from behind the bar. He leaned to his right and bent down like he was getting something underneath the counter.

"Oh, shit," I said.

The gunman turned his head toward Rocco. "Don't move arsehole," he said. But Rocco wanted to be the hero and started to draw his firearm. The gunman fired before Rocco even aimed. Rocco's body twisted sideways, his left hand holding his right shoulder, as his gun clattered to the floor.

"Any more cowboys?" The gangster asked, brandishing the gun around the room.

I stared. It can't be—how *could* it be?

I watched him climb over the beams and shards of glass toward our table at the back of the restaurant. As he came closer, he slowed down and eyeballed me under the table.

"Marie? Are ya okay, lass?"

"*Niall?*"

He got down on his haunches and said, "Aye. And you're a sight for sore eyes, luv. But I can't chat just now," he said and winked. "I've missed you, *mo anam cara.*"

My chest squeezed with an old longing as I scanned his weathered face and looked into his deep aquamarine eyes. I saw the reflection of a summer thirteen years ago in a small village in West Cork and a handsome fisherman who'd grabbed my heart and never let go. I saw us motoring to Fastnet Lighthouse, where we'd jumped off his boat naked and swam to the rock. I saw us pulling lobster traps, drinking Guinness in MacCarthy's Pub, and singing melancholy Irish songs that made my eyes tear. And I saw cool summer nights on a trawler covered in warm quilts and felt his soft tongue mingling with mine.

"It's not what it looks like, Marie. I'm being blackmailed. I was supposed to get Costello on my trawler and back to Ireland, or they'll blow my boat up with my lads inside."

I believed him. Niall was a kind man, always generous with his catches to those less fortunate. He was well-liked by everyone. I cannot believe he's ten inches from my face. I wanted to grab him and hold on forever.

And then I blurted out, "Take me with you."

He's surprised, but his smile is wide and happy. "Are you serious, woman?"

"I am. You asked me once, and I refused. I won't do that again."

"It's too risky now, luv." He hesitated, looking at me with a cool fire in his eyes.

"A'right. In two days, *The Irish Wake* will be waiting for you at six in the morning at The Fish Pier. You know where that is?"

"I do."

He squeezed my hand, then stood quickly, stepped over planks and broken glass, and bolted out the back door. Sarah stared at me in disbelief. I was ashamed that I was bubbling inside with happiness while all around me was pain and devastation.

"Is Rocco dead?" asked Sarah.

"No," I said. "Niall just winged him."

"What in God's name is going on, Marie?"

"I'll tell you later."

* * *

The piercing sound of fire engines, police, and ambulances died down after the police questioned everyone about the Irishman who'd aided in the failed escape of Red Costello. Costello was pronounced dead at the scene, and Rocco only had a flesh wound. But one of the patrons told police that the Irishman spoke to me. When asked what the Irishman said, I told him, "He just asked if I was okay."

"Why you?" asked the policeman.

Sarah quickly interjected, "Because he likes pretty girls?"

* * *

Emerging from the chaos, it was pitch black out, and a dozen cameras burst white in our faces. "Who was the Irishman—what was going through your mind in there—what did he say?"

Sarah started to tilt toward a microphone, but I pulled her arm roughly.

"No comment." I hurried up Cambridge Street as Sarah put her hand on my arm.

"Marie, wait a sec," she said, breathing heavily.

I stopped walking. "Look, I'll explain everything on the train. Are you alright?"

"Yes. I believe it's because I believe in the afterlife. That and the preventive worrying I do that keeps me in shape for the big stuff. You know, your Irishman is handsome in a thuggy kind of way."

I shook my head and kept walking. As we entered North Station, the smell of pizza and coffee filled the air. We stood waiting in front of the monitors and looked to see which track our train was on. Sarah tapped her foot impatiently and kept looking at me, waiting for the scoop. Ten minutes later we were sitting in the first car of the train, on the Rockport line.

I pulled my train pass from my tote bag when Sarah said, "You know what I was wondering back there?"

"How long it takes your body to decay?"

"Up to a week, but that's not it. I was wondering what the Irishman said to you in that funny language."

"*Mo anam cara.* It means my soulmate in Irish."

And then Sarah's cell went off. "Hello? Okay. Yes. Okay. Thank you."

"Was it Dr. Bazari?" I asked.

"Yes. It's a B-12 deficiency."

"Thank God. I can't take any more drama today."

"So, was he *the* Irishman?"

"Yes. His name is Niall Donnegan. After college, I decided to backpack through Ireland around West Cork, where my ancestors are from. I was only supposed to go for two weeks but I met Niall and fell in love with him. Three months later, I came home."

"Why didn't you stay?"

"Because I was young and scared. Niall was nine years older than me, and I thought it was just a summer romance. Unfortunately, I was wrong."

"Wow. All these years later, and he's *still* the one?"

"Yes. As soon as I saw him today, I knew. My life hasn't been the same since that summer. No matter who I've dated, they all seem like boys in comparison to Niall."

"So, you're really going to do this? Take a trawler to Ireland and go on the lam with a gangster until they catch you both?"

"Damn right. I know you think I'm out of my mind, but I'd rather have a few exciting years with Niall than live in a constant state of expectancy that, any day, something will happen, and it never does. Maybe someday he can clear his name."

"Hmm. You never know what's going to happen in life, do you?" asked Sarah. "I mean, who would have thought we'd have a near-death experience today? You know I only want the best for you, Marie. And here's what I'm thinking. If you would only believe in the afterlife, like the Druids, and somehow you get shot with Niall, then maybe you'll meet again on the other side." Her eyes were full of hope.

I waited to respond while I digested Sarah's theory. In a few days, I'd probably never see her again. What was the harm in letting her think she might actually be on to something?

"Hmm. Think I should start planning what to put in my coffin?"

Sarah's face lit up. "Yes!"

The conductor walked by, checking for passes while a man across the aisle, who smelled like he'd taken a bath in a barrel of whiskey, was snoring with his mouth open. As usual, the windows were dirty and the indentation of my seat was so deep I felt like I was sitting on a toilet bowl. The train jerked several times, and the drunk fell sideways. I leaned my head back and thought of Niall's eyes, swimming in the Celtic Sea, the green-green grass of Ireland, and how I'd never ever have to take this dirty, uncomfortable train again.

Meanwhile, Sarah pulled out the book, *Soul Survivor,* and began to read.

After a few minutes, I looked over and saw a large tear drop onto the page. She sniffled and wiped her nose with the back of her hand. I'll miss her too.

Wicked.

Keeping Abreast

Nothing traumatic ever happened to me while growing up, like having my spleen removed or getting my period in white shorts, in a canoe, on a first date (Sheila Troon, no lie). That is, until at the age of twenty-nine, I woke up with sixty-seven-inch breasts. There'd been no warning, no gradual swelling like a surfer's wave, just an overnight surge of tidal tissue submerging my former self.

My nightgown ripped open, revealing breasts so enormous that when I sat up, I had to hold one in each hand, then swing my body to the side of the bed. When I let go, they dropped to my thighs like two bags of potting soil, yanking my body forward until I nearly tipped over.

"Holy shit!" I hollered.

I lugged myself to the full-length mirror of my bedroom to take a better look. My chest reminded me of a map of the eastern and western hemispheres divided by the prime meridian. My moles and birthmarks resembled volcanic islands and landmasses, one of which looked like the map of Sierra Leone.

I trotted back to bed, my heart pounding like the hooves of a racehorse. Had I eaten anything different the night before? Taken any new medications? Was the hamburger I ate yesterday injected with a new hormone the farmers were testing? I was mystified by the absurdity of my situation and called my best friend, Evie, as the tears bounced off my boobs.

She came right over.

"Oh my God!" she yelled, unable to take her eyes off my chest. "You poor thing. Do you have a temp? A rash? What are you going to wear to work?"

"I can hardly walk, let alone go to work, Evie. Look at me. I'm hideous."

"We need to go to the ER," she said, marching toward the bedroom. "I'll get a sheet and wind it around you and put a blanket around your shoulders."

I mentioned it was eighty degrees outside, but Evie was on a mission.

In her car, I pulled the seat way back so my chest wouldn't mash against the dashboard. Evie kept looking at me sideways. "Are you in pain?"

"Ya-aah," I said, cradling my boobs each time we went over a bump.

***

Stooped over and taking small steps, I walked down the hospital corridor while people openly stared, as if privacy was only when you got a room with a curtain. Even the staff ogled me.

"These people are very unprofessional," I whispered to Evie. "How would they like to wake up like this some morning?"

Three hours later, they called my name, and I shuffled forward with Evie at my side. The doctor drew the curtain aside and said, "Hello. I'm Dr. Snyder. Let's take a look and see what's going on here."

He gently probed and prodded. It was terribly awkward and I've never felt so mortified and vulnerable. As the tears drizzled down my cheeks, I prayed I'd wake up from this bizarre nightmare.

"I've never seen anything like this, especially since the growth spurt happened overnight," he said, lifting each of my breasts. Focusing on the massive wart on Dr. Snyder's nose, I wondered why he'd never had it surgically removed. Then I thought of breast reduction surgery, thinking I'd be on the operating table for days.

Dr. Snyder leaned back and shook his head. "I don't know what to tell you, Miss Eikenberry." The sadness in his voice was so disheartening I whimpered like a newborn.

He put his hand on my shoulder. "You should make an appointment for breast reduction as soon as possible. I'll give you the name of a surgeon. He looked at me with a grim expression. "I'm so sorry I can't give you a diagnosis. Unfortunately, I'm as perplexed as you are."

When the door clicked shut, Evie and I sat in silence.

After a while, Evie said, "Come on, Nita, let's go." She helped me to my feet, and we left the hospital.

On the way home, Evie suggested getting another opinion. "Maybe there's a doctor in Switzerland who knows about this condition. People sometimes go there when they can't find a cure in the U.S."

"Yeah, sure, Evie. I'll just hoist me and the twin peaks on a plane to Zurich and let you know how I make out." I knew she was just trying to help, but her suggestion annoyed me, like there was some easy way out of this.

* * *

That night, I lay in bed thinking of my options. How would I ever learn to live with sixty-seven-inch breasts? If I had the surgery, would they grow back? And if I didn't have the surgery, would they grow even larger?

Then I wondered why some people elect surgery, and others don't. Fear? Affordability? I thought about the wart on Dr. Snyder's face. Did he feel it was part of who he was and didn't want to change what he'd been born with? Like Barbra Streisand and her nose, or the Russian leader, Gorbachev, with the map on his head?

It would have been nice to call my mother and ask her advice. But she would have waved me away. She's not all there, my mother.

I was the youngest of the Eikenberry brood, and it seemed Mother ran out of energy by the time I was born. When the five of us sat down in the high-ceilinged dining room of the large Victorian home we'd inherited from my grandparents, there was Big Daddy, with his overwhelming voice and opinions, and Mommy Dearest, in some far-off land who didn't even try to look interested. My older brother, Max, was a relief pitcher for the Pawtucket Red Sox, and Danielle, a former prom queen, was so wrapped up in herself she needed a bow. Scott, the closest to me in age and my favorite person in the world, still buys me little gifts like body lotion, chocolates, or one time a small flashlight on a keychain that I still use, even though it turned rusty years ago. I was a quiet kid, but Danielle always knew when I was upset because my face turned beet red, especially when Mother forgot to set a place for me at the table.

* * *

Still awake at sunrise, it dawned on me that Scott was a carpenter and an inventor of sorts. So far, it had only been mechanical tweezers and a hand-held snow remover for small areas. But clearly, he just needed more marketing experience. Maybe he could build some kind of boob walker that would ease my pain.

I called him on his lunch hour and explained the situation. Shocked by my sudden abnormality, he came to see what was going on. Lowering my sheet caused his eyes to pop out and his skin to redden from neck to hairline. I realized how weird and embarrassing it must be for him, but my modesty had taken a dive in the last twenty-four hours. He tried to hug me but he floundered and instead squeezed my hand.

"Aww, Nita. I feel so bad for you." His voice was so sincere it made me cry.

* * *

Three days later, Scott constructed a titanium walker on wheels with soft padded cups that I could raise or lower, depending on my position. The cups were stationed below my shoulders and above the steering handle so that each breast could be lifted and placed into the molds comfortably.

He'd also built a basket for my pocketbook and small purchases from the grocery store like milk and eggs, or bread and coffee. The best part was the collapsible umbrella he attached to the handlebar for rainy days.

"You'll look like a busty Mary Poppins," he kidded. I smiled, appreciating his efforts, but not quite ready to laugh about my situation yet. I was enormously self-conscious and hadn't been to work since it happened, calling in sick with a chest virus.

While trying out my new walker up and down the hall of my apartment building, I ran into my neighbor, Mrs. Hopper. I was wearing a yellow muumuu that belonged to Evie's grandmother. Mrs. Hopper stopped short and gave me a disgusting look.

"Look at you," she hissed. "Strutting around and showing off your humpty dumpties. You look like a whore."

I was too shocked to respond. How could she say something so hurtful? Calling me a whore because I had big breasts? Back in my apartment, I sat on the couch and cried until my breasts ached, as if they, too, had been insulted. Mrs. Hopper walked bent over and had three strands of hair left on her head. I could have called her an old bald bitty, but that would have been cruel. Plus, I didn't think of it at the time.

* * *

Although in much less pain with the boob walker, I was terrified of going out in public after Mrs. Hopper's comments. I made omelets until there were no more eggs, ate all the bread and peanut butter, finished the canned soups, and finally, the rest of the milk. All that was left was a crusted jar of honey, a tea bag, and some rice in a box.

Rather than go grocery shopping, I ordered a pizza. When the deliveryman arrived, he'd taken one look at my chest dropped the box, and the pizza slid out on my bare feet. "Ahh!" I yelled as hot globs of cheese and tomato sauce splattered my bare feet.

"I'm so sorry," he said, bending down to retrieve the box. "Are you okay?"

I kicked the box out into the hall, "Just go!"

"I'm sorry," he said, bumping into the doorframe as he backed out. Then he whispered, "Are those for real?" I slammed the door in his face then went and soaked my feet in ice water. Afterward, I made a cup of tea and boiled the last grains of rice.

Meanwhile, my boss called and asked if I had enough vacation days and sick time to cover my absence, to which I said, of course, thanks for asking.

The next day, the odor from the wastebasket overwhelmed me, and I couldn't leave the trash in the hall, or Mrs. Hopper would come banging on my door. It was a rubbish day, and I thought by going fast, I might get away without anyone seeing me. I wore another muumuu Evie had dropped off and hung the trash bag on the handle of the boob walker. I made it to the sidewalk just as the truck pulled up.

"Mornin'," said the trash man, trying not to stare. As I leaned over the handlebar to pass the trash bag, my right boob made a break for it. The man who'd been hanging on the side of the truck lost his footing and fell to the ground. I rushed back into the apartment building, holding on to the muumuu for dear life, and didn't leave the apartment for three days.

Soon after, Scott brought me a new shower apparatus he'd just built and a meatball sub. He sat down and put his hand on my arm. "Nita honey, you need to find a way to accept all this. Either that or change it. I hate to see you hiding and alone. It breaks my heart. Why don't you just have the surgery?"

I shook my head emphatically. "It makes me physically ill just to think about it."

"But you can't stay in your apartment forever." There was a plea to his voice that made my heart constrict. "You know, there's lots of people with worse deformities than you. Look at the elephant man." My eyes nearly popped out of my head.

"Come on, Nita, I'll go with you. We'll take a walk, and if anyone says anything, I'll punch their lights out."

He was right, of course, but it was hard to go from being a person of no interest to the lady with the jumbo jugs.

* * *

I took my first shower with the new apparatus, placing each breast in a rubber bowl attached to a mechanism that allowed me to rotate underneath the showerhead. It felt wonderful, and as the warm spray washed over me, I thought about what Scott had said, hating that he was upset by my lack of courage.

The thing is, if I wasn't going to have the surgery and wanted to live a reasonably normal life, there would have to be some changes. The first was to get rid of the muumuus and buy some good support bras. I found a website that carried them in my size and had them FedExed to me.

But the bras didn't do the job. My back still hurt from the weight of my breasts, and I was terribly sore by the end of the day. Scott went to work again, and within a week, I was wearing a bra that had wider, more comfy straps, which went over my shoulders and down my back to a soft cloth belt around my waist. The support was much better, and the weight was evenly distributed around my torso.

Next, I found a website that carried clothes with expandable bodices and empire waists. They came in tasteful, subtle colors and flattering designs.

On Saturday, Evie dropped by with chicken salad sandwiches. She told me it was important that I love myself in spite of the huge change in my appearance. She was making pink lemonade at the sink, and I was sitting at the kitchen table, figuring out how to tell her I didn't need her grandmother's muumuus anymore without hurting her feelings.

"You know, Nita," she said. "If you've chosen not to have breast surgery, you should name each breast as if they're your pets or children. That way, you'll feel less alienated from them."

"Hadn't thought of that."

"Well, I think Gwen and Jessie would be good. They sound warm and friendly, don't you think?"

I shrugged, then remembered how some women referred to their breasts as "the girls." I held them in my hands and realized it did make me feel more maternal towards them. Then I imagined breast-feeding and the baby gasping for air as it tried to gulp all the milk splashing in its sweet, innocent face.

* * *

Until I could work up enough courage to go out in public again, I resorted to watching *Discovery Channel*. In a chair with cushions mounted underneath my breasts, I watched it for hours. It put things in perspective, especially during Shark Week when a man's leg was bitten off. Huge breasts or one leg, I'd pondered. Huge breasts—no question.

After many self-pep-talks and deep breaths, I was ready to make a public appearance. Mrs. Hopper wasn't around when I took the elevator to the lobby. I walked to the street, passed by the library, and toward the playground, concentrating on the sidewalk so the wheels of my walker wouldn't jam in the cracks. It was a breezy June day with a bright sun, and no one seemed to notice me. I inhaled freshly mowed lawns and felt light-hearted for the first time since my transformation. I stood up straight with my shoulders back and pulled my stomach in. My new navy blue tunic and white capri pants made me feel stylish. Maybe I was ready to go back to work. And Scott would be so proud, which meant a lot to me.

As I passed the schoolyard, a young boy yelled, "Hey! Look at the boob, babe!" My heartbeat escalated. I walked faster. Then, I saw several other boys join in. They ran along the fence beside me, calling, "Boob babe, boob babe!" Their voices grew louder, taunting and teasing. They pointed and laughed, and their ridicule made me want to melt into the sidewalk.

I hunched my shoulders and put my head down, trying to shrink inside myself. Then, I felt an uncontrollable whirlwind of terror and difficulty breathing. The voices faded as the world spun around me, and I lost my sense of place. There was no way to calm down during the episode, which seemed to last forever.

When it stopped, the loud voices resumed. It took a minute to reorient myself and regulate my breathing. I looked at the sweaty, pimply faces of the boys, their scrawny, undeveloped bodies, and imagined that future generation of men.

And I snapped.

"You little dickheads," I snarled. "Boob babe, uh?" I scrunched up my face like a madwoman. "You want to see some boobs?" I lifted my top up over my bra. I bounced Gwen and Jessie, and the boys stepped back from the fence. "How 'bout this?" I turned to the side, still watching them with deranged eyes, and juggled my breasts one at a time. Then, I faced the fence. "You want more?" I growled. They shook their heads and backed away, staring at me with frightened eyes and open mouths. "Then go play your little boy games—and leave me the fuck alone!"

I swung my walker around and marched down the street. I had never lost my temper like that, and it felt marvelous to give it back and defend myself. I should have done that in sixth grade when the boys called me Velveeta Nita because they said I had a face like cheese.

Soaring with self-worth and confidence, I went to the supermarket. Outside, I donated a buck to the local girls' softball team and saw them nudge each other. But they didn't laugh and said thank you very much. I would get used to the staring as long as people were respectful.

In the store, while trying to reach a jar of strawberry jam, a man moved close to me. When I turned, he was staring at my breasts, his hand out as if to touch them. Turning back to the shelf, I flipped a plastic jar of peanut butter on his head, scaring the heck out of him. "Whoops," I said and moved down the aisle.

* * *

I soon realized I didn't have to hide from the world. I could be a part of it, but would have to continue to stand up for myself. I ordered more clothes and held myself in good posture. I used product in my wild and curly hair, even though Mother had called it maniacal.

Gwen and Jessie became my babies in the boob walker, and I proudly pushed us around town. My self-assurance must have been evident because men started offering to carry my bags and opening doors for me. I began to care less if people thought me a whore because people like Mrs. Hopper would always think like that.

A few days later, I went back to my job as Head Teller of the Walden Savings Bank, informing my manager that he couldn't fire me because I would sue for discrimination. He promptly transferred me to the drive-up window, where there was a stool, and I could rest my breasts on the counter. A few days later, he told me he noticed that the drive-up lines were getting longer, and people were opening new accounts like the bank was giving away cars. He winked and said, "Good job." Are you kidding me? This jerk had hardly acknowledged my presence in the past ten years, but now I was doing a good job?

Then I found an AA group, which stood for Abnormalities Anonymous, in hopes of meeting other people in my situation, well not exactly the same, but peculiar nonetheless. There were only a few of us at the first meeting, and everyone sat in a circle. The leader's name was Odin, and he had a long gray braid and one dangling peace sign earring. He asked us to say our names and tell the group why we were there. I thought it was obvious but soon found out that abnormalities aren't always apparent.

Roger, a middle-aged man with a paunch that toppled over his belt like an avalanche, said that he woke up one morning without a navel, completely gone, stomach smooth as a baby's bum.

"I looked down the bathtub drain, emptied the hamper, stripped the bed, and checked the disposal," he said. "Then I searched my drawers but never found it. I wondered if it had dissolved back into my stomach. The doctors couldn't tell me why it went missing, and it's still a mystery after six years!"

The group shook their heads in sympathy. Odin nodded as if this was an ordinary occurrence and moved on to Martin, an accountant at the IRS, who smelled like sour milk and could only speak backwards. He went to a neurologist, a neurosurgeon, and a speech therapist, none of whom could diagnose his problem. "Life in alone very feel I," he tried to explain in earnest.

Finally, there was a pretty teenaged girl named Louise. Well, pretty if you didn't count the hay growing from her nose and ears. It happened during her senior year of high school, just before graduation. Odin had to coach her to talk she was so embarrassed.

"Every night, it grows another six inches, and I have to cut it right before school, then rush home before it starts again like I'm a she-wolf. An ear, nose, and throat specialist looked up my nose and in my ears. But she couldn't find the root of the problem even with a CAT scan." Louise put her face in her hands and sobbed, "I don't want to live like this!"

I listened to their stories with great empathy, putting myself in their position instead of dwelling on my own. We all met for coffee afterwards, four of us squeezed into a booth by the window like a bunch of society's outcasts. There is nothing like being in a support group with others who share the same kind of issue. And to my surprise, I found myself offering advice and encouragement.

I told Roger, the man without a navel, that sometimes we never learn the answer to things like who really killed JFK, for example. To the man who talked backwards, I said it would force other people to listen more, and wasn't *not listening* a major problem in this world? (Although, the sour milk smell was probably the main reason he was alone.)

To the girl with hay growing from her nostrils and ears, I suggested that she donate the hay to science and make good use of her impediment. It must be a rare kind of hay and could contain a compound or protein that would be beneficial in curing a disease.

"For instance, I once read that placenta—you know the stuff that comes out when a woman has a baby? Well, that's used for treating obesity and heart damage." Hay girl had looked at me strangely but I could tell she was considering it.

I knew then that it was my destiny to help others who were different, those who didn't fit society's standards, and the real reason for my transformation. Because I, Nita Eikenberry, finally had something to offer the world—and it was empowering.

* * *

I began conducting seminars and held workshops calling my new business "Aberrance is Awesome." Eventually, word spread, and I was soon presenting talks on a national level. One day I was even invited on *Day to Day* with Susannah Curry. Susannah couldn't take her eyes off my chest and kept saying, "Oh my."

I tried to smile, but the heat from the bright camera lights caused a sweat pool between Gwen and Jesse. Susannah asked if I'd sought a second opinion on my "condition," she called it, clearing her throat.

"At the time," I answered, "I was overwhelmed with fear and embarrassment. Just going to the Emergency Room was an ordeal. So, seeing other specialists didn't appeal to me." The more I talked, the easier it became. "Over time, with help from my brother, a close friend, and a support group, I gradually became less frightened to go out and live my life as an epic-size-breasted woman."

"Well, I give you a lot of credit for coming on the show and sharing your, may I call it metamorphosis?"

Ever so graciously, I said, "Yes. But, of course, I'm not a giant bug now, am I?"

She put her hand on my arm and said, "No, no, of course you're not."

***

A month later, I appeared on *Mid-Night with Johnny Mallen*. He made me laugh, kneeling in front of me and bowing with his hands outstretched, calling me, "Nita, Queen of All Women." I was wearing a gold sequined dress and matching gold heels and felt glamorous. He asked me about my boob walker, who had made it for me, and I was thrilled to tell him about Scott. I even gave the audience Scott's website address.

I thought my parents would be proud of me, but they weren't. Neither was Danielle or Max. Asked to visit, we all sat in the front parlor of the family home. The sun cast a warm glow across the Oriental carpet. To an outsider, it appeared to be a friendly family gathering. But it was far from that.

My father started the conversation with a fake cough, while my mother's eyes never left my chest. Danielle texted the entire time, and Max looked spellbound by my physicality.

"First of all, Nita," my father began, "None of us understand this condition you have. However, be that as it may, we must try to make the best of the situation. It's been very difficult for your mother and I, not to mention your siblings, to see your unfortunate transmutation on television and magazines. Max's teammates make crude remarks and want to date you." More fake coughing. "Danielle is asked why she doesn't have your boobs, hooters, whatever you want to call them. Therefore, I am willing to pay for your surgery and the subsequent doctor bills so that you can live a normal life again. But!" He paused dramatically. "If you don't agree to this, we demand that you move away and change your name."

"Are you on board with this, mother?" I asked, stunned.

She nodded yes, but her eyes were vacant. "Still that maniacal hair," she murmured from another universe.

"And you, Max? Danielle? Where is Scott, by the way?" I asked.

"He was not invited," my father said sharply. "And yes, Max and Danielle agree. Now, what's it going to be, Nita?"

Heartbroken, I refused to cry. I stared at each member of my family. What was wrong with them? Did I have to fit some kind of acceptable category, be a pro athlete or pretty, to be loved and respected by my own family? Were they really that shallow?

"You guys suck," I said, rising from the sofa and grabbing my boob walker. "I never did like any of you."

No one said goodbye. No one asked if I needed help down the stairs to the sidewalk. When I looked back at the house, my mother was at the window, peering through the sheer curtains. What was she thinking? Was she even capable of thinking?

* * *

Now, karma being what it is, payback came when Helen Genest invited me on her show. I told her that my entire family, except for Scott, had disowned me because of what they called my unfortunate transmutation. Tears filled Helen's eyes. The camera spanned the audience and some of them were outright crying. Sitting on stage with Helen, I was reaching people like myself, but also the Mrs. Hoppers of the world who had wrongly judged me.

Meanwhile, Scott was building devices left and right, finally making the money he deserved. His target market expanded to canes for the handicapped with flashing lights, walkers with alarm systems that alerted the lame from ten yards away, and a fake navel for Roger made from silicone. He bought a house on Lake Prospect with a detached garage where he could create more inventions.

I was working on a book called *A Titillating Tale of Transformation and Triumph* and had already received a large advance. I bought a sprawling bungalow, and Scott built ramps at the front and back doors.

Soon, abnormal people started appearing everywhere. Photos appeared in the media of people with two thumbs, one lip, double kneecaps, and no elbows, arms flailing at their sides.

One day, I had an idea for a parade similar to the Gay Pride Parade, only I called it the Personal Pride Parade. Two hundred people marched down Main Street, supporting the need to be accepted in a world striving for perfection. There were cameras everywhere and all of us smiled, even those who had never grown teeth, which was a real breakthrough for them.

As we approached Town Hall, I saw Danielle and Max in the crowd. They were carrying a sign that said, WE ARE VERY SORRY, NITA. PLEASE FORGIVE US. The guy from the pizza delivery was there as well as the trash men, Odin, Dr. Snyder, Evie, and Scott. Even Mrs. Hopper was there. My eyes filled, and my heart burst with love and forgiveness. Then I saw Mrs. Hopper's sign: 'YOU'RE STILL A WHORE!'

And I laughed.

Dear Ruth

I stood at the kitchen counter, knowing I shouldn't open another one of her letters. Yet, here I was, tearing the envelope open and soaking up her every word—in a letter to a dead woman.

Dear Ruth,

Hello again from Ireland. I'm still here at the Slea Head Writers' Retreat, working on a short story collection. There's no television or internet access here so I'm living like a hermit with clean sheets.

Are you receiving my letters or tossing them in the rubbish like you did with my less-than-stellar stories? They've never been returned so I assume you're just busy. I often think of you in your splendid home and the cozy parlor where we discussed who better than Nabokov could write about pedophilia as artfully as he did in Lolita.

The tranquility and beauty here is astounding and I'm slowly finding that "distinctive, wry voice" you missed in my more serious works. Perhaps the dry wit of the Irish is rubbing off.

Thank you for kicking my butt these past few years, even though you made me cry. Did you know that? Don't worry, I'm over it. Mostly. Since I'm 3,000 miles away I can tell you that and not fear your wrath, oh mighty mentor.

I hope you're well, Ruth. I miss our perfervid discussions (how do you like that one?), and just in case you're yearning for my voice, my cell phone number is 617-xxx-xxxx. Remember, I'm five hours ahead.

Your devoted student,

Rachel

The boldness in Rachel's letters intrigued me because I'd never had that kind of free-spiritedness she shared with my mother. I remember when Mother first showed me her work.

"Jakob," she'd said, handing me the manuscript, "There's a new student in my workshop. You'd do well to write a brief as well as she writes stories," she said, raising her eyebrows.

Naturally I was offended, but after reading the first paragraph, I was more interested in Rachel than my mother's thoughtless comment.

> *I was wearing my Marilyn wig and a tight yellow pantsuit that pulled across my fanny like an ace bandage. The wig wasn't sitting right on my head, and I could feel the cashier staring at me. She had three hickeys in a circle on her neck and I wondered if they gave them out in patterns now.*

I'd laughed out loud. But Mother was also very tough on Rachel, and one night, I heard her yelling on the telephone.

"Why are you writing these serious pieces when you have such talent for writing humor? Where is the girl I compared to Geoff Dyer?

I'd wondered if Rachel would cave or put up a fight and went to the door to listen. She'd pushed back because I heard Mother respond, "I don't want you trying anything else. The literary world has enough anguished writers and their tortured journeys. Stick to the humor!" Then she'd hung up. I assumed that was when Mother made her cry.

I knew I had to tell Rachel the truth. That Mother disappeared seven months ago off the coast of Cape Cod. What I wouldn't tell her was that I'd become oddly attracted to her from her letters and a photo of both of them on my mother's refrigerator.

When I heard her voice, my heart jumped.

"Hello. Is this Rachel Butler?"

"Yes."

"Rachel, this is Jake Dante, Ruth Dante's son."

I heard a low groan. "Is it Ruth?"

"I'm afraid so. She was swimming at our summer home in Wellfleet and never returned."

"Oh God. I'm so sorry. When did it happen?"

"Seven months ago."

A long pause ensued. And then I heard her blow her nose.

"Was I that far down on the call list?"

"Not at all. She thought the world of you. I had to wait for the Coast Guard, patrol boats, and helicopters to finish searching for her remains. Because she was so well known, there were tons of private boats that joined the hunt long after. Even then, I still held out hope. Finally, I had her declared officially dead this morning."

"They still haven't found her body?"

"No. Unfortunately, the sharks were rampant last summer, and we think she was attacked and drowned."

Her voice cracked. "Oh, Jesus. Why would she go swimming when there were shark warnings?"

"I told her not to, but she insisted, said she just needed to get wet. Swimming was like religion to Mother, and you must know how difficult it was to tell her anything. "

She didn't answer.

"How did you know where to find me?"

I looked up at the ceiling. "I read your letter."

"Oh. My last one?"

"All of them."

Again, there was a long pause and I waited in agony.

"That's a bit weird. But thanks for calling."

The line went dead, and I stood there staring at the phone. Then I threw it across the room.

* * *

Two weeks later, I called her again on a Saturday afternoon.

"Rachel, it's Jake Dante. Please don't hang up."

Silence.

"I know you think I'm despicable for reading your letters and not telling you about Mother sooner, but —"

"I used the word snake, but despicable works."

"Yes. I suppose it does. I hope there's some way you can forgive me."

"Not unless you tell me you had amnesia for what, seven months?"

"No. I didn't have amnesia. I didn't call sooner because I didn't want your letters to stop." I waited as beads of sweat broke out on my forehead.

"They were that riveting?"

"To me, they were. I never had the kind of relationship you had with Mother. I was very curious about you, and your letters kept her alive a little longer for me. God knows it was wrong, but can you understand that?"

"I guess, but I don't know what God has to do with it."

"Well, I hope someday you can understand that's not who I am."

"Who are you then?"

I twisted my Harvard Law ring. "I'd like to think I'm a good person who put off doing the right thing for selfish reasons."

"I'll think about it."

At least she was talking to me.

* * *

Fifteen years ago, Will Abrams and I were law students at Harvard. Now and again, we meet for lunch or a quick drink. Will works in the General Counsel's office at the State House, and I'm a defense attorney in private practice. Today, I was meeting him at *Grotto* on Bowdoin Street. He waved from the back as I squeezed through the room to a wooden booth.

"Looking good, *Jaay-kob*," he said, rising to shake hands.

"Cut the shit," I said. He knows I hate that name.

"Okay, okay. But let me ask you something. Do you notice how many women give you the eye? Be honest."

"I don't know. Maybe sometimes."

"What the hell are you waiting for?"

I could say I was smitten by my mother's protégé, who was ten years younger than me, but he'd never let it go.

"Gisele Bundchen," I said, signaling the waitress and pointing to Will's beer.

"Hah! It's good to see you, Jake. Everything settled with your mother's estate?"

I nodded.

"Maybe now you'll have some closure."

"Maybe."

* * *

In one of Rachel's letters, she mentioned she'd be home in early June and could she and Mother meet in Harvard Square, where she still bopped around every Saturday. Beginning the first week of June, I began scouting the Square, hoping to run into her.

The second week, I almost missed her as she walked into the Harvard Coop Bookstore. I followed her in, pretending to read the jacket of one of Lee Child's novels while watching her. She looked beautiful: thick brown hair pulled back in a loose ponytail, healthy natural complexion, and dark, playful eyes. I dropped the novel, bent down, hoping she wouldn't see me, and put the book back. Then I circled the store and walked quickly to the front, where I hid behind a bookcase like a damn gumshoe, waiting for her to leave.

"Rachel?"

She looked up perplexed—then she saw the likeness.

"Jake Dante."

"Yes."

She held out her hand, and we shook politely, as if I'd never read her letters, as if I'd done the right thing when Mother disappeared. The blood rushed to my face in embarrassment.

"When did you get back from Ireland?"

"A few days ago."

There was an awkward moment before I said, "Do you have time for a cup of coffee?"

I could see she had mixed feelings not that I blamed her. But I was her closest connection to Mother and figured that's why she agreed.

In Harvard Square, everyone was milling about, up and down the streets, in and out of stores. A street musician played *Eleanor Rigby* on his guitar, and Rachel tossed a dollar in his case. We strolled to Peet's Coffee and sat outside in the sunshine, facing the common across from Winthrop Square.

"You have Ruth's green eyes."

"So they say," I said.

"How did you recognize me?"

"My mother has a photo of the two of you on Cape Cod at her writing workshop. It's on the refrigerator in the kitchen."

I could tell she was surprised.

"I told you she was fond of you." She looked away, blinking rapidly.

"How are *you* doing?" she asked.

"I go through the motions, but her death troubles me, the way it happened—could I have done more to stop her?"

"I'm sorry. That's a heavy load. Was she depressed or troubled that day? I know she was heartbroken when your father died."

"She was lonely, yes, but do you mean…"

"I don't know what I mean. I just keep wondering *why*?"

The word hung in the air like a microscopic germ. We sipped our coffee and watched a group of teenagers lounging on the grass of the common, texting and laughing.

"The first time I met your mother, she told me, 'You have a distinctive, wry voice, but you need polishing.' I was so excited when she took me on. For the next two years, she taught me more about writing than anyone I'd ever known. I wrote a children's story once about flowers who talk, and she said, 'Stories that make inanimate objects real make my teeth hurt.' I was completely crushed."

"She was a taskmaster, for sure."

"Yes. But I would have run bald and naked to Race Point Lighthouse if she'd asked. Whenever I write I hear her voice, "Use contractions in dialogue, fiction is about what people do to each other, where is the conflict?"

"I can still see her pointing at me before I left for Ireland, that gold link bracelet she always wore flashing in the sunlight. "Don't come back until you find your voice," she said.

Rachel was lost in her memories of my mother, and I drank my coffee in silence. After a while, she said, "You're a lawyer, right?"

"Yes."

"Why a lawyer? And don't tell me it's because you can't sing or dance. "

"I'm a defense attorney, and I like being a hero."

"Seriously?"

"Sure. It makes me feel good when I save the little guy."

She smiled. "Do you live close by?"

"I used to. But I sold my condo and moved back to the family home in Brookline."

"I have so many memories of that house. I always loved the high ceilings and curved staircase."

"That's right. You've been there."

"Many times."

Rachel seemed relaxed, even during the pauses in our conversation. But I still needed her to know that it was not depravity that drove me to read her letters.

"I'm sorry for what I did, Rachel. I was kind of messed up for a while. You think you and I could have lunch sometime or meet again for coffee? We got off to a lousy start, and until now, our conversations haven't been exactly lighthearted."

"And I thought we could discuss quantum physics today. Clearly, you know more about me than I do you. What was it like being the son of Ruth Dante?"

I took a sip of coffee, holding it in my mouth before swallowing. I needed to be careful and not crush her adoration of my mother.

"Most of the time, my mother wrote or read, and she didn't like to be disturbed, so I used to hole up in my room and read the *Master and Commander* series and make model ships. I studied hard, went to Yale and Harvard Law, became an attorney, and here I am."

"No marriage or children?"

I shook my head no, rotating my class ring.

"What about your father?"

"The epitome of the old-school Harvard professor: bow tie, tweed jacket, a bit of a stuffed shirt, really, until my mother walked into the room. Then his face lit up. "Ruthie!" he'd say. "Come give me a smooch!""

Rachel gazed blindly into the distance. "I didn't know my father. He left when I was six. My brother and I started suspecting in high school that there was something wrong with our mother. She was sweet, naïve really, and I loved her dearly. But even when the phone rang, she looked distressed, like she might have to make a life-or-death decision. My aunt finally had her tested, and she was diagnosed with early-onset Alzheimer's."

"I'm so sorry. Is she still alive?"

"No. She died three years ago."

"I'm sorry. Where's your brother now?"

"He moved to Australia after she passed, and I haven't seen him since."

I didn't want to seem over-eager, but neither did I want the afternoon to end. Ever.

"My mother let me read one of your stories. She told me I'd do well to write a brief as well as you wrote a short story."

"Ouch," she said.

"Yes, ouch. I laughed like hell when I read it. She was right. You really do have a flair for humor."

"Just hearing you say that makes my shoulders tense," she said.

"Why?"

"Because the more she pushed, the more I lost my timing and spontaneity."

I nodded, knowing how hard Mother could push.

We left Peet's and strolled through Harvard Square, our faces flushed from a hot June sun. We browsed the kiosks, where she bought a copy of *The Paris Review*, and I grabbed the *New York Times*. Students with backpacks sped by on bikes, and others sauntered hand in hand, some with green spiked hair and Gothic eyes or complicated tattoos that flaunted their individuality. At dusk, when the Square became shrouded in orange and pink hues, Rachel said, "It looks like a village in a fairy tale."

And I felt like a king—but I didn't tell her that.

* * *

The following weekend I invited Rachel to the house in Brookline for dinner. When I opened the door, she was gently touching the wind chimes on the porch. What memories did those chimes bring back for her? I led her down the hall to the parlor, where she immediately sat on the couch across from the fireplace, as if that's where she'd always sat.

"Red or white wine?" I asked.

She was looking at a framed photo of my parents and me on the boat in Wellfleet. I left the room and came back with two glasses of chardonnay.

"Are you okay?"

She nodded and lifted her glass, but her eyes were moist. "Cheers."

"Cheers. Have you been through the whole house before?"

"Yes, it's magnificent but I wouldn't want to clean it. Something smells good; what is it?"

"Veal Marsala and roasted rosemary potatoes."

"Oh yum."

Then she roamed the room. On a table by the window were more photos of a young Ruth with Truman Capote and Kurt Vonnegut, receiving the Pulitzer for *The Trouble with People*, and standing at the shoreline in her bathing suit and wearing a flower petal bathing cap. In the large gilded mirror, Rachel looked at me with mournful eyes, and I felt like melting chocolate. She looked away and paused at the bookcase, then stared at the Edward Hopper paintings, at a ship hull mounted on the wall, at the books unevenly stacked on every spare tabletop, tilting her head to read the titles.

"It's as if she's still here," she said.

* * *

At dinner, I watched in awe as she devoured the veal, sopping up the juices with a baguette and dribbling it on her chin.

"What?" she asked when I smiled.

"You eat with gusto. It's fun to watch."

She wiped the gravy from her chin with a napkin and said with her mouth half-full, "I bet I look like a ranch hand spooning chow by the campfire."

I burst out laughing and said, "Great visual."

After dinner, in the living room, I talked about living in Brookline as a teenager. "A family of eight lived across the street and reminded me of the Kennedys. I'd listen to them yelling and laughing while they played touch football in the backyard. Sometimes, I smelled weed floating from their upstairs window. They had these white toothy smiles, and I'd watch them hop into their Beamers wearing Harvard sweatshirts and Ray-Bans. I was taught to take life a little more seriously."

"Really? But Ruth had such a marvelous sense of humor."

I tried not to let my expression change, but she caught it.

"Was she different as a mom?"

"Yes."

"How so?"

I frowned and rotated my ring. "It's not something I like to talk about. Another time, maybe. How's your writing coming along?"

She started to say more, eyed my expression, and stopped.

"I *was* writing short stories for a collection, but after you called, I kept thinking of Ruth. Then I started jotting down notes, anecdotes of our relationship, snippets of our conversations, and how a fledgling writer caught the eye of one of the country's most famous authors."

"You're writing about Mother?"

"It's an homage, Jake. I want to be humorous about how I couldn't write humor after being noticed for writing humor."

I paused, looking at her sitting on the couch surrounded by my mother's nebulous presence. "You should write it here, Rachel, where she lived and wrote."

She looked around the room and rubbed her arms.

"I work all day so they'd be no interruptions. The house could be your muse."

"I don't know, Jake, it seems like such an intrusion of your privacy, and hers."

"I wouldn't offer if I didn't mean it."

She bit her bottom lip, and her dubious expression turned to excitement. "Are you absolutely sure it wouldn't be an imposition? Maybe I could just come for a few hours in the afternoon?"

"Absolutely."

She had no idea how much I would love to come home and find her here.

* * *

Sometimes, she was gone by the time I got home, and my disappointment was palpable. Other times, when I would see her beat-up Corolla in the driveway, I was filled with pure joy. Then I would go to the market, where I bought groceries, hoping she would stay for dinner. When she left, I felt alone and couldn't wait until the next time I saw her. Often on weekends when she needed a break, we walked along the Charles River, or saw an Indie film at Kendall Square and had dinner at Legal Sea Foods. I wasn't sure if I was a friend or a boyfriend. I hoped it was the latter.

We grieved together albeit in different ways. I, in my often-quiet spells, filled with sorrow and missed opportunities, and I imagined Rachel in her memories of my mother's teachings and loyal guidance.

* * *

By late fall, our relationship finally turned a corner. There'd been several times when I wanted to kiss her, but I was afraid of rejection. I didn't want her to think she owed me anything. I was that insecure about her feelings for me. One night, by accident, she turned at the door, and I was right behind her. I bent down and kissed her gently on the lips. She kissed me back with much more passion than I'd expected. When we broke away, she said, "I've been wondering when you were going to do that."

"I wasn't sure you'd let me."

We made love until dawn. There was nothing hesitant about Rachel. She was loving and passionate, and she provided me with the warmth and happiness I'd been craving all my life.

I was so happy I was nervous. One night, I asked if she loved me.

"I believe I do," she said without hesitation.

"Why?"

"Why?" She crossed her arms and stared at me for a moment. And then she said, "I love you because you're not afraid to show your vulnerability. You're thoughtful, intelligent, and quite dashing."

I felt a tidal wave of happiness flow through my body. "Want to know why I love you?"

"No."

"I love you because you're funny, kind, and genuine. And you are the loveliest woman I have ever known."

Her face turned bright pink. "Alrighty then. Glad that's over with."

* * *

Several nights later, I was shaken awake. "Wake up, Jake," Rachel whispered. "Wake up."

"What's wrong?" I mumbled.

"You were yelling in your sleep."

Disoriented, I turned over. "What did I say?"

"Please don't, Mother."

I pulled her into the curve of my body, staring at the model ship I'd made on the mantle, wondering if Mother would approve of Rachel in my bed.

Two nights later, it happened again. "Mother...stop...just stop." I woke crying and felt Rachel's arms around me.

"It's okay, Jake. It's okay."

In the morning, I told Rachel that I'd been taking anti-anxiety medication after Mother's disappearance, but stopped because I didn't want to become dependent.

"You can't just go cold turkey, Jake, you need to wean yourself from those."

I knew she was right, but I didn't want her to think I was weak. It was a colossal mistake.

* * *

Rachel used her humor to help me relax, something she said she'd resorted to all her life in times of pain. She put a wreath of baby's breath on her head and marched into the room, stating she had a summons from Caesar. She crossed her eyes in the midst of a serious discussion. One day, she stood at the counter with her back toward me. When she spun around, she was wearing glasses with a big nose and a mustache attached.

"Care for some coffee?" she asked.

"Rachel. You make me so happy."

* * *

A week later, after another sleepless night, I spilled a pint of cream all over the counter and yelled, "Son of a bitch!" Then, in one fell swoop, I swept the recipe books, jug of wooden spoons, the knife rack, and the toaster off the counter and onto the floor. Rachel stood up to help but I screamed, "NO!" holding my hand up like a traffic cop.

She backed off and watched in silence as I wiped off the counter, cleaned every appliance in the kitchen, and returned everything to its proper place.

"Sorry."

She looked at me with a mixture of wariness and confusion.

"What's going on, Jake?"

I put my fingers to my temples, trying to clear the clatter in my head. "I don't know. These memories of my mother keep resurfacing in my dreams."

"Like what?"

I sat down sighing, and began winding my ring furiously. I told Rachel things I wish now I hadn't.

"I was twelve years old when Mother first told me I was a mistake. That she and father had decided early on they didn't want children. They had each other and that was enough. But they calculated wrong and their prearranged future was disrupted.

I was helping her dig a hole in the garden, and she thought it was funny, but it explained why she hardly ever talked to me. She once introduced me to her friend saying, 'This is Jakob, my biggest mistake,' and they both laughed." And I just stood there like a ninny.

"No," said Rachel.

"I know you loved my mother, and this is hard to hear. But the thing is, she didn't have to raise you or love you; she could mentor you with very little emotional commitment, and you would be the proof of her success as a teacher. That's what Mother did best. You could only get so close. She was like taffy, pulling away yet leaving you painfully attached."

"I don't know the woman you're talking about, and I don't understand her behavior with you, Jake. Obviously, her death has caused you a lot of pain. Did you go back on your medication?"

I shook my head no.

"Then you need to talk to someone. You can't go on like this, babe."

"I know. But I can't change the past, and that's what's torturing me. I'm late for court. I'm sorry." I left her there sitting at the table. I couldn't focus all day afraid she'd think I was unhinged."

* * *

When I got home that night, her car was there, and I was elated. Rachel loved me. She would stick by me no matter what. I'd go back on my medication, buy her a new BMW, we could marry, have our own children, and I would be a nurturing parent. I fumbled with the keys to the back door and walked through the house, calling her name.

She wasn't writing in the parlor or anywhere else downstairs. I heard something on the second floor and ran up. Rachel was sitting on my bed, staring at my mother's gold link bracelet in the palm of her hand. The second drawer of my bureau had been pulled out and was leaning precariously forward.

"I always loved this bracelet," she said. "It seemed part of her, like a birthmark. She told me she never took it off, not even when she swam, because Nico gave it to her on their wedding day. Why do you have this bracelet if your mother disappeared?"

The bracelet lay in her hand like Exhibit A in the State vs. Jake Dante. Her eyes showed no mercy, only a vacant stare. And then she started crying.

"Please tell me what I'm thinking isn't true, Jake."

"Rachel. I can explain." I sat down on the bed and she slid away from me.

"What really happened?" she asked, her eyes pleading as the tears drowned her face.

"She called and wanted me to come to Wellfleet. All my life, I'd always hoped the day would come when Mother and I could simply talk—without argument, without criticism. Just talk, you know?"

Rachel looked at me without the love I'd come to depend on, and I prayed with all my heart I could make her understand.

"We were sitting at the kitchen table, and Mother was going off about this guy whose yacht was blocking her water view. She was on the Cape Cod Beautification Board and was starting a petition to stop this guy from ruining the waterfront with his big fancy boat. She wanted me to represent the Board and bring the guy to court.

"We'll sue him, Jakob. I'll write an article for the *New York Times,* and we'll stop this damn narcissist from invading our coastline."

It was like her last hurrah. She wouldn't let it go and kept telling me I had to do this for her. Maybe I just wanted to say no to her for once in my life.

"What's the matter with you? Where's your fight?" she screamed.

"I asked her to please stop. But she was mad as hell. Then she stood up and leaned over, her face two inches from mine. "You're nothing but a poor man's lawyer with no balls!"

"I needed to get away from her and shoved the table as hard as I could. Her chair and the table flipped over, and she fell back, cracking her head on the ceramic tile. I never meant to kill her. I swear to you. But she was eighty years old and more fragile than I realized."

"Why didn't you call the police and report it if it was an accident?"

"I panicked. There was so much blood from her head wound. The table was knocked over, and it looked like an assault. I'm her sole heir, and it was no secret that my mother and I were not close, therefore I had motive. I'm a lawyer. I know how these things work."

"What did you do with her body?"

I played with my ring, then said, "I waited until dark, then I tied her in a tarp with cement blocks from under the porch. I placed her in the dingy tied up at the dock, and drove out to Ferry Island where the seals hang out. Then I slipped her over the side into the water."

"Oh my God." Rachel put her face in her hands.

* * *

It was a long, long time before she stood up. Her eyes were red, and her face blotched. While I watched, she reached into the pocket of her jeans, pulled out her cell, and dialed 911.

* * *

It's been two years since I was tried and found guilty of second-degree murder. Rachel returned to Ireland, where she continued to write. I'd always wondered how she felt after they led me away, but I never heard from her again until today when I received her package.

Inside was the book she wrote called *Dear Ruth*, with an inscription.

> *For Jake—*
> *The hardest thing in life is to walk away from the person you love. To betray that person is harder still—even when it's the right thing to do.*
> *RB*

The Madness of Ida Mae

(Previously published in 2014 by Bryant Literary Review) Finalist for the Al Blanchard Award

I stood in line at Stop & Shop in my Marilyn Monroe wig and a tight yellow pantsuit that pulled across my fanny like an ace bandage. I'm almost eighty years old, but when I wear a push-up bra and one of my movie star wigs? Ain't nobody I can't charm. My wig wasn't sitting right on my head, and I could feel the cashier staring at me. Her nametag read Lulu. It suited her.

"Do you have a Stop & Shop card, Ma'am?" Lulu asked, looking at me with bored dungeon eyes. Her purple hair sprouted from her head in different lengths, which made her look like a porcupine that fell into a paint bucket. The bullet holes in her ears were turning green, and she had four hickeys in a circle on her neck. I wondered if they gave them out in patterns now.

"Why, certainly," I said, pulling the card from my wallet. "I never leave home without it! You know they have polish you can buy for jewelry."

"Excuse me?"

"I said they have silver polish you can buy for those earrings. I use—"

"I heard you the first time, lady, and I like my jewelry just like it is."

"I'm just sayin'. You wouldn't believe how new it'd look if you wiped it off with some Bling Brightener, takes two seconds."

Lulu ignored me and snapped a bag open like a firecracker, throwing in my Ben & Jerry's ice cream, a bag of Lay's chips, and a pound of Oscar Mayer bacon.

"Careful there, Lulu. Don't be smashing my chips."

"Have a nice day," she said, rolling her eyes as she turned to the next person.

"You too, *Lulu*," I said. Girls today look like vampire sluts.

When I got in my car, I pulled down the visor and checked my face in the mirror. One of my fake eyelashes was crooked, and I had lipstick on my teeth.

"Fuck it," I said and flipped the visor back in place.

* * *

Six months ago, my husband, Wilfred, moved in with the hostess at Kon Tiki Liki out on Route 1A. I figured he needed to squeeze out the last drops of man juice before he dried up. Of course, it's only a matter of time before he comes back. Wilfred and I have over fifty years together and I know he wouldn't throw that all away.

Wilfred's sex slave was a younger woman in her late sixties named Vera. I knew her from the restaurant and always thought she was a floozy. She never looked at me when she took our order, and when she asked if we wanted anything else, she used to raise her eyebrows at Wilfred. Vera and Wilfred took our dog Brando with them, which was fine with me since Brando used to pee on the plant in the hall, and, like Wilfred, he had bad aim. But I would never ever divorce Wilfred; I'm just waiting 'till he's done making an ass of himself.

I live alone with my Siamese cat, Jackie, in Summerfield, Massachusetts. I named her that because she looks like she's wearing big, round sunglasses. I always loved Jackie Kennedy even after she married Ari, the Greek shipping guy with the bags under his eyes. After Wilfred moved out, I bought two wigs: my Marilyn Monroe and my Liz Taylor. When I wear them, I pretend I'm a seductive starlet, not some lonely old broad whose husband walked out on her.

I've got a ten-room purple Victorian on a street that backs up to reservation land and some scary wildlife. One day, I was taking out the trash, and on the way back, I looked straight into the eyes of a coyote. I ran like the dickens and damn near lost my Marilyn in the driveway.

Wilfred and I bought the house five years after we were married, and I was still working for the phone company. The house needed work, but it was solidly built and had a nice staircase and mahogany banister. I used to throw our dirty clothes over the railing because the washer was off the kitchen. Wilfred didn't like that because sometimes his underpants would land on the banister.

Over the years, we added a garage and had all the hardwood floors redone. Wilfred made a brick patio in the back where we used to drink lemonade and eat Ritz crackers with slices of Cracker Barrel cheese on top. I wanted to get the little Black boy carrying a lantern for the front lawn, but Wilfred put his foot down on that one. I told him I don't have anything against the Blacks. I just love that lawn ornament. Wilfred said that wasn't the point. So, we got the pink swans on sticks that I call Dick and Liz, but Wilfred said we had to put them out back.

* * *

The phone was ringing when I got home. I had to put the ice cream and bacon away, so I let it ring. Wilfred's voice came over the machine, and my hand stopped midair.

"Hello, Ida Mae. Are you there? Pick up if you are. Okay, guess not. I'd like to stop by tonight and pick up my father's rocking chair for my studio apartment."

Studio apartment? What, he's a painter now?

"I was thinking maybe around seven o'clock. Can you call me back when you get this message?"

I looked at the clock. It was 4:30. If I started the tub now, I could take a bath and change into something sexy so Wilfred would see what he was missing. My new pink halter top came to mind. I was hoping Wilfred wanted to come back and was using the rocking chair as an excuse. I'd heard from Flo, the teller at the bank, that he and Vera had broken up.

Wilfred arrived in his new Prius and seemed right at home, sitting at the table with his legs crossed, looking around the kitchen. It reminded me of all the times we'd sat there together over the years. I'd made coffee and put out a plate of Oreo cookies for us.

"I'm leaving early Thursday morning and driving to Rangely to catch some fish," he said. "I may stay overnight, I don't know."

"That's nice," I said, flicking off some non-existent lint from my pants.

"You and Jackie seem to be doing well," he said. Wilfred and Jackie never got along mostly because she used to puke in his Rockport's.

"We're doing fine." (The worst thing a woman can do is let a man know she's needy.) "Jeremy's mowing the lawn, and if I need him for odd jobs, he comes right over," I said. I leaned over and scratched the back of my neck, nudging my breast with my arm, so it popped out a bit.

"He's a good kid," Wilfred said. He took a sip of coffee and stuck his pinky out like he always did. "Have you met the new neighbor across the street?" he asked.

"Yes. But I'm too busy to bother with foreigners."

Wilfred looked confused.

"She's a Ruskie, Wilfred. Her name's Mawi or Mari. I can't understand a word she says."

"I would think it'd be nice for you to have another woman living nearby."

"We have nothing in common," I said, adjusting my Marilyn and fingering the pearls Wilfred had given me on our last wedding anniversary.

"She's a widow, right?"

I nodded. "Does she have any kids?"

"She mentioned two sons who I think she said were living in Tibet, but she might have said Dedham."

The truth was I'd been watching her since the day she moved in. I knew something funny was going on because a big woman with hair cut like a soldier came to visit her every weekend. I'd never known any lesbians except for Ellen and Rosie, but I was pretty sure that's what they were. The house was set back from the road, and I planned on buying binoculars so I could see closer. But Wilfred didn't have to know everything. I believe women are more attractive when they have secrets.

"So, did Vera dump you?" I asked, rearranging the sugar packets in the ceramic holder.

"Absolutely not," he answered.

"I just thought she'd want someone her own age," I said.

"It wasn't that at all."

I bent over to pat Jackie, giving Wilfred another chance to see my bosom.

"You know Ida Mae," he said, pausing and giving me the once-over.

I sat up a little straighter.

"Yes?"

"It's been six months. You really need to do more with your life. Look at me. I've got my own place, I'm off fishing, planning my next adventure. Instead of sitting around reading movie magazines and wearing lopsided wigs, why don't you lose some weight and have that front tooth straightened? Who knows—there might be someone out there who'd like a companion."

I almost threw the plate of cookies at him. I jumped up, grabbing his cup and saucer, and went to the sink. I started rinsing the dishes, then spun around and said, "And who the hell do you think you are, Cary Grant?"

Wilfred let out a sigh and stood up.

"You know, I thought maybe we could have a nice conversation, Ida Mae. But I see that's impossible. You're still the same woman I married fifty years ago. Every time I've ever tried to help you, you lash back at me," he said.

"Well, then, why don't you keep your big trap shut?"

"Is the chair still in the basement?"

"Yes."

"And why do you still eat that junk?" he said, pointing to the Oreos. "No wonder you move around like a cripple."

"You used to eat Oreos all the time."

"People change, Ida. Don't you get it?"

* * *

"Son of a bitch," I said, slamming the door after him. *What are you eating that junk for, Ida? Why don't you do something with your life?* Because I like my life, okay? So did you once upon a time. Oh, but not now—now you're twenty pounds lighter and think you're Mr. Wheatgerm."

I took three eggs from the fridge. Then I went outside and stood on the patio. One by one, I threw the eggs at the old maple tree. They splattered as they hit the bark, and I watched the yolk run down the trunk.

"Asshole," I said and walked back into the house. I took off my Marilyn and scratched my head.

"Should've made hot dogs wrapped in crescent rolls with a slice of cheese in the middle. He loved those."

* * *

When Wilfred left me, I ordered a framed picture of Jackie Kennedy in New York City, crossing the street with her hair blowing across her face. I hung it on the wall of my bedroom. Then I bought a full-length mahogany mirror so I could stand in front of it and do imitations of Liz and Marilyn.

When I wear the Marilyn, I sing, "Happy Birthday, Mr. President," in a whispery voice. And when I wear the Liz, I do a scene from *Butterfield 8* and say, "Mama, face it. I was the slut of all time."

I can't believe how much I sound like Liz Taylor.

Every morning, I have coffee and eat frosted cinnamon buns in the dining room while I watch the house across the street. The house was vacant for two years on account of the old coot that lived there died, and the kids were fighting over his estate. It's one of those white antique capes with green shutters, a stone foundation, and a nice front porch. It's real quaint and reminds me of those lake houses in New Hampshire where you sit on the front porch at night and swat mosquitoes.

Sometimes, I watch my neighbor from the second-floor guest room, where I peek through the curtains, hardly moving them really, and kneel down on a thick pillow with my elbows resting on the sill. I feel it's natural to want to know what another person does all day long. Besides being a lesbian, I wondered if Mawi had some crazy habit, like dressing up like a priest. I read about that in the *National Enquirer*. Some woman dressed up as a priest in

Billings, Montana, and tried to hear confessions at church. She called herself Father Toni.

One day, I got Mawi or Mari's *Home Improvement* magazine by mistake and had to put it in her mailbox. I rummaged through her other mail, but there wasn't anything good. I'd ordered binoculars from LL Bean and couldn't wait for them to arrive so I could see through her sheer curtains. It would help fill the days until Wilfred came to his senses.

After the binoculars came, I found out that every night after the eleven o'clock news, Mawi sits at her kitchen table, drinks a cup of tea, and smokes a cigarette. She rinses out her cup and saucer, runs the cigarette under the tap, then puts it in a paper towel. After that, she throws it in the wastebasket, the kind you step on, and the top flies open.

On weekends, soldier girl visits, and they sit together at the table smoking and talking. One time, I was watching them smooch at the table. I swear to God, soldier girl almost swallowed Mari's head. Then they went upstairs, and I couldn't see what they did after that.

I miss Wilfred a lot. But frankly, I'm really not interested in making new friends at my age or in some guy who's looking for a mother. Besides, I want to stay available for Wilfred. On the other hand, if a George Clooney look-alike showed up selling Jesus, I could be persuaded to drop a few pounds and get a bikini wax. I think I'd wear the Liz for George. I've got a feeling he likes brunettes.

* * *

The next time I heard from Wilfred was three weeks later. I'd been sweeping the backstairs in my denim mini skirt and when I walked in the house, I saw the light flashing.

"Hello, Ida Mae. It's me, Wilfred. I've decided to move to Kansas and buy a small farm. I'd like to come by the house Sunday and say goodbye if that's okay with you."

Goodbye? For good? I was stunned. What happened to the studio apartment? I felt like I'd been hit over the head with a bat and swallowed a handful of dust from under the couch. All I'd heard from Wilfred was a check in the mail since the last time he came over. I called him sometimes late at night but hung up when he answered.

I dialed his number and got his machine.

"Hello, Wilfred, it's Ida Mae. As if you didn't know my voice. Anyway, so you're moving to Kansas? My goodness, Wilfred." I paused, thinking of something I could say that wouldn't sound desperate. "Well, if you'd like to come for supper, I could make something." I hesitated while I tried to swallow. "I could make maybe a meatloaf or franks and beans with some nice warm brown bread or something. Let me know so I can go to the grocery store. Okay. Goodbye. Call me back. Okay. Bye, Wilfred."

I looked out the window at the brick patio that Wilfred had made so long ago. Kansas was a long way away. How could he go that far away when he still loved me? Especially since I was starting a new diet next week. I'd even made an appointment with my dentist to get my tooth fixed. He couldn't just walk out of my life like this. It didn't make sense.

I had to do something to stop him. Wilfred had always thought he was smarter than me, but I wasn't as dumb as he thought. He used to love jigsaw puzzles, and instead of talking to me, he'd spend hours at the dining room table bent over the damn things. He didn't even say thank you when I made him coffee and served *Nilla* wafers. When I sat down to watch, he said I was jiggling the table. After he'd gone to bed, I took Jefferson's nose from the Mount Rushmore puzzle. He went crazy looking for it but I've still got it hidden in the bottom of my jewelry box.

Kansas. What the hell was he up to? First, it was the floozy, then the studio apartment, and now Kansas. Wilfred didn't know what he wanted.

* * *

I wandered from room to room, rearranging things, then looked out the window to see what Mawi was up to. She and soldier girl were just getting in her car. I needed to get my mind off Wilfred and decided to go over there after they left to check things out.

It took me longer than I thought to get to the backyard and climb the small hill behind the house. I felt a little dizzy when I got to the top, but sure enough, I could see straight into the bedroom with my binoculars. If I came back at night, maybe I could see them having sex! I'd always wondered how other people had sex. I used to feel like I was paying the gas bill. I wondered if that meant *I* was a lesbian. I laughed nervously all the way home. And Wilfred thought he had an exciting life.

When I got in the house, I called Enzo's Pizza and talked in my Marilyn voice. "Hi. I know I sound just like Marilyn, but it's me, Ida Mae."

"Well, I thought Marilyn had come back from the grave! What can I do for you, Ida Mae?" asked Enzo.

I giggled. "I'd like a large pizza with onions, garlic, pepperoni, and sausage. And can you deliver that to four Larch Road? Thank you *so* much."

After lunch, I checked on Mawi and saw her and soldier girl carrying a bag of groceries, trying to get in the front door. I wondered what was in the bag. Probably cabbage leaves and beetroots for that soup the Ruskies make. I hadn't made soup in years, but Wilfred used to love my beef stew.

* * *

That night I waited until after they had their cigarette and tea then I dressed in black jeans, a black sweater, and a black stocking hat. A full moon, like a movie camera, lit up the yard as I slid against the side of her house. I tripped on some rocks going up the hill, but I had a perfect view of the bedroom because they hadn't pulled the shades down, and the light was on. Panting, I sat down on a low, thick tree branch.

I raised my binoculars and saw Mawi standing in her bra and panties. Soldier girl was topless, and for a big woman, her breasts looked like two flat pancakes. I must have moved because before I knew it, the branch snapped, and I tumbled forward and slid down the hill. I screamed and tried to get up, but every time I got to my knee, I fell over. By this time, Mawi and soldier girl had come outside, and I thought they were going to hurt me.

"What the fuck you are doing?" asked soldier girl.

Mawi said, "It is neighbor, Mrs. Jacquith."

* * *

I was shaking when I finally got back on my feet. "I'm very sorry," I said. "I thought my cat got out and came over here."

"*Bazdmeg*," said the soldier.

"Thank you," I said.

Then, I limped across the street as fast as I could.

* * *

When I got home, I was all wound up. Mawi's girlfriend had scared me. I was thinking about Wilfred and what would happen to me if he moved away for good.

By dawn, when I still couldn't fall asleep, I got up and made coffee. I peeked through the curtains, wondering if Mawi and soldier girl believed my story about the cat. I'd been pretty quick with that one. Wilfred called back around nine but said no to dinner.

"Thank you, Ida, just the same but I've too much to do before I leave. I'll be over around three o'clock. Okay?"

"I guess. I still can't believe you're moving, Wilfred. It seems so sudden."

"Actually, it's not. I used to talk about moving to the Midwest to all that wide-open space, maybe have a small farm and live off the land."

"I don't remember."

"Well. I'll see you around three o'clock." Wilfred said.

He sounded so happy I felt like punching him in his privates. Instead, I went into the living room and took the picture of us on the pier at Old Orchard Beach in Maine and bashed it against the mantle.

* * *

Wilfred looked like a twit in his cut-off jeans, Birkenstock sandals, and wool socks reaching kneecaps that needed facelifts. His thin gray hair was parted from the top of his left ear up over his bald spot and down to his right ear, where it looked like it was plastered to his head with rubber cement. The Grateful Dead T-shirt with the teeny holes in the armpit was the topper.

I'd taken pains to look casual yet elegant. I had on white linen pants and an oversized red silk blouse with a wide silver belt. I wore the Liz wig with silver hoops and a pair of red slippers. Then I applied bright red lipstick, going outside the lines to make my lips look bigger.

Wilfred jumped when I opened the door.

"What the hell?" he said, looking me up and down.

"Fuck you, Wilfred. If you're going to make fun of me, then you can turn around and march right out the door!"

"Why do you need to use the F word?" he said.

"Emphasis, Wilfred. Are you coming in, or are you going to stand there on the stoop like an encyclopedia salesman?"

Wilfred stepped into the hall. "I wanted to say goodbye and get the camping equipment from the attic. I don't suppose you'll be using it anymore?"

"You never know," I said, thrusting my shoulder out, trying to be flirtatious.

Wilfred gave me a strange look and walked into the living room.

"I see you're still wearing your wigs," he said.

"Why wouldn't I?"

Wilfred shrugged and sat down. He leaned over and folded his hands between his knees.

"Can I get you some lemonade, Wilfred? I made some an hour ago, so it should be nice and cold."

"No, nothing, thank you." The doorbell rang. "Were you expecting someone?"

"Well, no but I've been involving myself more with neighborhood activities," I said.

I opened the door, and Mawi and soldier girl were standing on the front stairs. I gasped when I saw my binoculars in Mawi's hand. Soldier girl was peering at me like she wasn't sure if it was me or not. Last night, I'd been wearing my Marilyn. Wilfred came up behind me and leaned over my shoulder, trying to see who was there. I tried to block him, but he moved forward, extending his hand.

"Hello. I'm Wilfred Jacquith. Are you the new neighbor?"

"Yes. Mari Bashmet and Petra Harkov."

"How do you do." Turning to me, Wilfred asked, "Aren't you going to invite them in?"

"Come in," I said curtly.

"No," said Petra. "We go out."

"Yes," said Mari, holding out the binoculars. "We came to give binoculars wife left in back yard last night."

"What?" asked Wilfred.

"Never mind, Wilfred. Go sit in the living room," I said.

But Petra wouldn't let it go. "Tell husband what you did."

"Never you mind. Thank you for the binoculars," I said, trying to shut the door.

"What's going on here?" asked Wilfred.

"Your wife spy on Mari and me in bedroom."

"Oh Ida," Wilfred said.

* * *

"Okay, that's enough," I said. "You people need to leave." I shut the door.

Wilfred looked at me. "What is *wrong* with you?"

"Shut up. There's two sides to every story, and I can't go into my side right now." I lowered my eyes and said, "I don't want to hurt anyone." I guided him into the living room. "Please. Sit down."

Wilfred sat down in his old chair, looking depressed.

"How about some of that lemonade now?" I asked.

"I don't want your lemonade, Ida. I don't want anything to do with you."

"What?"

"I want to end this relationship. I want a divorce."

Divorce? I'll be a divorcee? Oh God. I took a deep breath, trying to stay composed.

"Now, Wilfred, don't go making any quick decisions," I said, swallowing, my heart hammering and my face burning like a fireball.

"How could you spy on the neighbor like that?" he asked, looking at me as if I'd stabbed a kitten. "Don't you have any decency?"

"I told you—you don't know the whole story."

"It doesn't matter. You're only going to lie to me like you did when you started that petition to keep that Iranian family out of town, telling everyone they were recruiting terrorists from our daycare centers."

"That was different, Wilfred. I was being patriotic."

"You're out of control, Ida Mae, and I want no part of it anymore. It's time we made our separation permanent.

"I see," I said, but not really. I was sweating like a mechanic, and the word divorcee kept ringing in my head. I could feel the fried pastrami I'd had for lunch creeping up my throat. It took everything I had to remain calm.

"Are you planning on remarrying?" I asked, burping. "Pardon me."

"No."

I thought about crying, begging him to stay. But then I thought of Jackie Kennedy and what she would do.

"So, how does this work?" I asked. "You move to Kansas, and what, we do this all by mail?"

"Yes, precisely."

"I see," I said. He'd thought it all out, the bastard, probably had a self-addressed stamped envelope in his pocket.

And then I had another idea. "I must say, Wilfred. It's one thing to want to spread your wings, but divorce is an entirely different matter."

"I'm sorry. I need to make a clean break."

"Naturally, I'll want more money," I said.

"Why do you need more money? I've been very generous with you, Ida."

"Well, I wasn't too sure where things were headed, but now I'll need to get myself a good lawyer and make sure I get everything I deserve."

"Now, let's try and do this amicably. I don't want it to get messy."

"Oh, it's going to get messy, Wilfred," I said, looking away. "You can't just walk out on me and expect me to go along with everything *you* want. I have a stake in all this, too," I said, swooping my arm around the room.

"Well, it's still fifty-fifty in Massachusetts. You're not going to get any more than you're entitled to."

"We'll see, Wilfred," I said.

Wilfred exhaled like it was all too much for him. "I'm going up to get the camping gear in the attic," he said.

I nodded. My outfit, the calm demeanor, the scare tactic, none of it had worked. He was never coming back. I couldn't think straight and felt like I was going to faint.

A minute later, I heard him yelling from the top of the stairs, "Ida Mae! Where are the poles that go to the tent? It's not with the other stuff."

"How the hell should I know?" I hollered back. Like I'm going to help him leave.

"Well, would you mind getting off your fat ass and helping me look?"

Fat ass? Is that what he'd just said? I couldn't believe he'd be that hurtful. I'd stood by him through that whole Vera thing and waited while he acted like a fool. Whenever he came over, I tried to be friendly and go out of my way to have something he liked. I could've thrown something at him when he made that crack about my tooth. But I didn't.

I stood up, opened the drawer of the end table, and then marched to the staircase, seething. The attic door was open and I could hear Wilfred banging around up there.

I'd never been so mad at him, even on our honeymoon when he laughed at my thighs. Did he stick up for me in front of the Ruskies like I would have done for him? No! All he ever does is criticize me. So, I've made a few mistakes in my life. Who hasn't? When I reached the top landing, I paused to catch my breath, still holding on to the banister.

"It's a miracle you can even make it up here," said Wilfred, shaking his head from the top of the attic stairs.

I looked up at him through a yellow haze of dust and mites. Then I raised my eyebrows and smiled. Wilfred looked at me oddly. Still smiling, I pulled a key from the pocket of my pants, stepped back, and locked the attic door.

"What the hell are you doing, Ida?" he screamed, his words muffled by the thick oak door. I could hear him pounding against it, but the house was old with good bones, and the two small windows in the attic were double-paned and painted shut. No one would ever hear him.

* * *

I was still smiling as I slowly walked back down the stairs. In a few days, Wilfred would settle down. And then I wouldn't hear him at all.

Laughing, I went into the kitchen and turned the oven on to three hundred and fifty degrees. I was dying for a bacon and cheese meatloaf.

The Domino Effect

On Thanksgiving Day, 1966, in a small town in Western Massachusetts with a large population of French-Canadian immigrants, Henri Levasseur sits in a rocking chair that's been in the family for years. His right foot pushes the chair gently back and forth while he watches Ada at the stove. Thick, strong hands clasp across his wide stomach as he circles his thumbs, a longtime habit of contentment. His jaw juts out, which makes him look stern, but his heart is as big as the kitchen he rocks in.

Henri closes his eyes, loving these quiet moments before the house fills with the voices of his daughter-in-law, Connie, and his three grandchildren: Debbie at twenty, home from Harvard where she won a full scholarship, Ridley at eighteen, a football star and senior at the local high school, and Anne at sixteen, a junior at the same school. Henri says a silent prayer that his son, Richard, will not ruin another family dinner as he has so many times before.

Ada has been trying to teach Anne to sew. Sometimes, she comes over after school, and Henri drives her home. But Anne is impatient and often clumsy. Ada tells her, "Take your time, dear. You'll do better if you just slow down."

Henri had snapped the newspaper, catching Anne's eye and winking. Her problem is not that she rushes. It's that she's trying too hard for her father's approval. When Anne got a C in Latin, Richard made her quit drama club, where she was rehearsing as the lead role in *My Fair Lady*. Anne was devastated and, soon after, began having stomach aches. She couldn't understand why her father was being so hard on her, and she was rattled by his decision. It was the first time she had ever received a grade that low.

"Please, Daddy, I promise I'll bring my grade up next term."

"You say that now, Anne, because you want something, but how do I know that for sure?"

It was as if he didn't trust her. She was confused by his behavior. She went to her mother and pleaded with her to change her father's mind.

"I'm sorry, Anne. He's your father, and what he says goes."

Then, three days later, Richard changed his mind and said he was sorry. But it was too late. They had already replaced Anne in the lead role.

* * *

"Henri, did you put the chairs around the table?" Ada breaks into his thoughts, and he automatically rises, straightening his arthritic body.

"Yup. Do it right now."

He takes the chairs from the kitchen table and lifts them under his arms into the dining room. Henri always sits at one end, and Ada sits at the other. Anne insists on squeezing next to Henri because she adores him.

Henri walks back into the room and says, "All set. What else do you need me to do?"

"By now, I'd think you know," she says, in that schoolteacher's voice he doesn't like. Although Ada was a good woman, she'd been a strict mother to Richard. Her own mother had passed away at a young age, and Ada had become the mother to her four siblings when she was only thirteen.

"Put the table pad on and get the tablecloth from the linen chest," she says, not looking up as she stirs the chocolate pudding for the cream pie.

"Yup," he says again, then whistles a tune with no melody.

Since Henri retired as a linesman for Western Electric, he drives his grandchildren around because Richard and Connie only have one car, and Richard takes it to work at Bramley's, where he's managed the produce department for the last three years. It is the longest time he's ever held a job. Connie knew he loved stirring the pot and got himself in trouble, especially with those in authoritative positions, like his mother or his bosses.

It doesn't take much to make Connie happy. A buxom blonde, she wears her hair similar to Marilyn Monroe and enjoys cleaning her little ranch home, hanging laundry on the line in the fresh air, and reading Victoria Holt novels. Each night, while she makes supper, she sings along to whatever's on her small kitchen radio, swinging her hips to the beat.

Connie married Richard when she was pregnant with another man's child. Although she'd later miscarried, Richard would forever be her knight in shining armor. She knew about his first wife, who he'd found in bed with his best friend a month after they were married. Ada once told Connie that Richard's first wife's adultery had traumatized him. From then on, he'd seemed less trusting of people in general. It was a double blow because he had also been classified 4-F due to poor eyesight when he tried to enlist in the army.

He changed after that and began to drink, often becoming disrespectful and unpredictable. In those days, seeing a psychiatrist was unheard of unless you were seriously mentally disturbed. Ada had read an article in *Reader's Digest* about a man who developed a false bravado to cover his pain and insecurity and knew the same thing had happened to Richard.

Before they wed, Ada also told Connie he cared for her deeply and felt Connie had helped him. Connie doubled her efforts to be a good wife and stand beside him no matter what. Even when he drank.

* * *

On Saturday mornings, Henri takes Anne to her waitress job at the local diner. Richard and Connie aren't aware that as soon as they drive down the hill, Henri stops the car and gets into the passenger seat. Anne slides behind the wheel, and Henri lights up the forbidden cigarette, blowing the smoke out the window like he's on a road trip.

An aerial view of Henri's car traveling through town would show a gray Chevy Impala going forty miles an hour around corners, up over the curbstones of quiet tree-lined neighborhoods, stopping with a jolt at lights, or going straight through them. It's the only time in Anne's life when she feels free of any conflict. When they get to the diner, she parks with one wheel on the sidewalk and runs in to grab Henri a coffee and chocolate honey-dipped doughnut.

* * *

"Henri! Get the telephone!"

He rises from the chair. Picking up the black rotary phone that sits on a small table with a lamp, a pad of paper, and a pen for messages, he lines up the mouthpiece.

"Hello."

There's a slight pause then Henri says, "That's fine, Richard. See you when you get here."

"Who was it?" Ada hollers.

Henri moseys back into the kitchen and stands near the stove. Ada pours the rich chocolate into the golden pie crust with perfectly fluted edges and his mouth waters.

"Richard," he says. "The Thanksgiving game ran late, and Ridley needs to shower before they come. They'll be a half hour late, he says."

"How was he?"

"Upset."

Ada frowns. Why does Richard get so upset about things? He'd been a good child, but sometimes it took a paddle on the bum if he sassed her, or cried too long because the kids made fun of him. She gave him the sticks and stones adage and told him to ignore them. But he was only one of a few children who wore glasses, and the other kids called him four-eyes and Mr. Peepers, making a cruel circle around him.

Henri, on the other hand, was old school—he provided for the family financially—and let Ada take care of the house and their son.

* * *

Henri walks back to his chair and resumes rocking. "Better late than never," he says.

"Easy for you to say. You don't have to worry about the timing of the turkey and vegetables."

"It'll be fine, Ada. You couldn't ruin a meal if you tried."

She's quiet after that, turning the oven down and wiping her hands on her apron, the blue and white gingham Henri bought her at the church bazaar ten years ago.

Henri closes his eyes and thinks of Ridley, tall with black hair and black eyes. Both he and Richard are big men — although Ridley is taller. He's a superb athlete and is being scouted by the Big Ten universities. Henri worries about Ridley and knows he's smoking the pot because he can smell it when he gets in the car. When he dropped Ridley off at home the day before, Henri had said in a calm but firm tone, "Hold on a minute, Rid."

He put the car in park and turned to look at his grandson, whose head nearly touched the roof.

"If I find out you been smoking the pot again, I'm telling your coach."

"What?" Ridley said, unable to hide his surprise. "I don't smoke pot!"

"Don't lie to me, son. You smell like a skunk when you get in the car. I may be old, but I'm not stupid. I don't understand why you do it when there's a scholarship on the line. Especially right before you go home."

Ridley put his head down. "It's no big deal, Gramps. It just helps me relax."

"Why do you need to relax?"

"There's a lot of pressure on me right now, and Dad doesn't help. He's always on me every friggin'…sorry."

Henri noticed Ridley clenching his fists. "Smoking pot isn't going to help the situation. You've got less than a year to go, and then you'll be away at school. Hang in there."

"Yes, sir," said Ridley, red-faced. "But…

"But what?"

"You have no idea what it's like at home." Ridley had jumped from the car and slammed the door before saying more.

Henri sat in the car and watched Ridley go into the house. There's no way he would have told his coach, but he's aware of how difficult Richard can be and worried about how hard he pushes his children. Henri pulled away, a feeling of helplessness washing over him.

When Ridley and Debbie were kids, they used to try and pull one over on Henri. They thought he didn't know they took the pimento out of the olives, stuffed it with sugar, and put the pimento back in.

"Here, Gramps, have one," Ridley would say, trying to keep a straight face. They'd pretend to watch television, lying on the rug and sneaking looks at him. Henri would eat the olive and then ask for more, which made them roll on the carpet, covering their mouths and giggling.

He thinks of Debbie and his stomach still turns to mush. Two years ago, she found out she was pregnant. If Richard had known, who knows what he would have done? He still recalls when Richard grabbed her by the arm like a rag doll and lifted her from the table when she didn't say, "*Please* pass the potatoes." The dents from his fingernails in her arm lasted for weeks. She was ten at the time. Richard made her sit in the living room for the rest of the meal. She was so upset that she peed on the couch. He'd had four scotches in him at the time.

Debbie, being a critical thinker, wonders why her father drinks so much. Her mother is kind and keeps a nice house, the kids are all achievers, and he's kept his job for a long time now. She is unaware of his first marriage, or that he'd been unfit for military duty.

Debbie is a straight-A student who shows exceptional skill in Behavioral Sciences. But she made a mistake with the wrong guy during her first year of school. She turned to Henri and asked him for six hundred dollars for an abortion. She knew of a compassionate doctor who performed abortions in a safe setting. A friend, who came from a wealthy family, told Debbie her father paid a lot of money for her sister's abortion, but it was all hush-hush.

Henri had read in the newspaper about the horror stories of botched abortions. He was sick with worry. Could they trust this doctor? What if something happened and Debbie died? He would never forgive himself. But she was sobbing, and his heart twisted in pain. Torn over his love for Debbie, and his fear if something went wrong, he didn't sleep for days.

Ada sensed something was going on. "Henri, why do you toss and turn so? Did you have cheese before bed?"

"No. Just one of those nights."

In the end, Henri drove Debbie to the clinic and told Ada he was going fishing with his friend from the diner. He wanted to see the clinic and meet the doctor before the procedure. Slightly reassured by the immaculate setting and professional manner of both the doctor and the nurse, he paid the doctor from the money he borrowed from St. Bernadette's Credit Union. Ada would never know because they normally did their banking at Berkshire Bank & Trust. He tried to read magazines in the waiting room, but his hands were shaking, and the words blurred on the page.

Debbie was groggy when she came out. The nurse told Henri that she might have some cramps. But Debbie smiled and hugged Henri fiercely, waiting a long, long time before she let him go.

"I'll pay you back, Gramps, I promise."

Henri took a handkerchief from his pocket and wiped the tears from his eyes, shaking his head no.

There were no complications. No one ever knew except Debbie and her grandfather what happened that day. Yet, he is still awake some nights because of it.

* * *

"Henri! Help me take the bird out of the oven."

Ada opens the oven door, and a whiff of hot roasted turkey floats from the oven. Henri lifts the pan easily. His hands are rough and calloused but still strong after years of climbing telephone poles. He sets it on the counter and puts a dishcloth over the meat.

"Did you wash your hands?"

"Twice," he says.

"Henri."

They hear four car doors slam outside in the driveway. The voices are high-pitched, and everyone is talking at once. Up the steep stairs to the second floor, they climb and cross the deck to the back door of the two-family house that Richard grew up in.

"See if they need help, Henri."

"Hi, Gramps," says Anne, who comes through the door first, gives him a big hug, then whispers, "Got a chocolate honey-dipped for you. Give it to you later."

Next is Debbie who says nothing but hugs him so tight he has to catch his breath.

"We're trying to get through the door, Deborah—move it," Richard growls from behind her.

"Hello, Dad," says Richard.

"Hello, son. You look well," Henri says and grasps Richard's elbow as they shake.

"Hi, Gramps," says Ridley. Henri can tell Ridley hasn't smoked the pot by the way he looks him straight in the eye.

"Rid. How's it going?"

"Good."

Connie is last and gives Henri a peck on the cheek. "Hi, Dad, it's good to see you."

Each of the grandchildren head toward Ada and tell her how wonderful everything smells. There's a flurry of activity as they take their coats off, and Henri brings them down to Richard's old room and lays them on the bed.

He hears Richard taking charge. "Ask your grandmother if she needs help, Anne. Ridley, make sure there's enough chairs around the table."

Debbie notices her father taking charge and how much he enjoys it.

"Oh, and *Deborah*." She winces at the way he says her name. "Tell your grandparents the big news," he says.

Debbie frowns. She doesn't want to make the announcement because she knows what will follow. But she can't ignore her father. He's already had a few drinks before they left, and any confrontation will mean a huge scene and ruin the whole dinner.

"I was told I have an excellent chance of being accepted to the Department of Behavioral Psychology, PhD Program."

"Which means she'll be a Ph.D., not an M.D.," Richard says.

"It's still a doctor," says Ridley.

"Watch your tone," says Richard. "It's not the same."

Ridley gives his father a dirty look, but his father doesn't notice. Here we go again, he thinks. Nothing's ever good enough unless he says it is. Ridley feels protective of Debbie, who works her butt off yet never gets any credit. And Anne, who means no harm to anyone, seems to always get the brunt of his cruel mouth. So often, he just wants to smack his father and tell him to wise up. He knows he could take him if he really wanted to and has dreams of him and his father getting into a brawl.

"Oh, my word," says Ada. "Can they still call you doctor?"

"Yes," says Debbie.

"What exactly will you be studying?"

Deborah pauses trying to think how she can make it simple. "I would be focusing on the science of human behavior."

Henri comes back from the bedroom and walks over to Debbie. "I'm so proud of you, Debbie," he says, putting his hand on her shoulder.

"Her name is Deborah," says Richard. "Why do you always use nicknames with the kids? You never called me Dick or Ricky."

Ada says, "That was my choice, not your father's, Richard."

"Figures," he says. "Anyway, Deborah still has a few years to go. By then, maybe she'll smarten up and become a real doctor."

"What can I get you, Connie? Richard?" asks Henri.

"I'll take care of it," says Richard as he pulls a bottle of scotch out of a paper bag.

"I'll get some glasses," says Henri.

Ridley tells everyone that there are now nearly five hundred thousand troops in Vietnam, and support for the war is decreasing every day. Richard tells Deborah her mini skirt makes her look cheap, as he pours a double shot of scotch into one of the glasses. Ridley wants to tell him Debbie could never look cheap but holds his tongue.

"It's what they're all wearing now, honey," says Connie. "And she has tights on underneath."

Richard gives Connie a warning look and says, "Makes her look easy." No one says anything. No one ever says anything.

Henri thinks of what Richard would say if he knew Debbie had an abortion and feels his heart clench.

"Gram, look what Mom bought me yesterday," says Anne, twirling around the kitchen in a colorful new pair of bell-bottoms. "How do you like them?"

"They're okay. But we could make them a lot cheaper." Ada has been frugal since the Depression when she made cupcakes, and Henri sold them door-to-door.

"I know," Anne answers, then accepts the glass dish of cranberry preserves Ada has put up.

"Set this on the table, dear."

Connie and Richard sit in the living room, watching the Macy's Day Parade and sipping their drinks.

Suddenly, Richard leans forward and says, "Wow! Look at the size of that float! Hey kids, come see the Superman float! How long do you think it took to make that? Wonder how much it cost to build. I bet it gets a prize for the best one. But what if the wires break, and he really flies up in the air, uh?" Richard bursts out laughing.

"Oh wow," says Anne. "That's really something."

Debbie agrees.

"Ridley—what do you think? Outta sight, uh?"

"Yeah, unreal."

"You don't seem excited."

"I am. It's pretty wild, Dad. Really cool, never seen anything like it."

"Are you being sarcastic?"

"No. It's really impressive."

Deborah folds her lips in, knowing Ridley is making fun of their father.

"Okay, everyone," calls Ada from the kitchen. "Dinner's ready."

Henri is at the kitchen sink, pouring scotch down the drain, then diluting the bottle with water. By his third drink, Richard will not know the difference. Ada sees and nods.

Ridley starts the dinner conversation while passing the rolls, "Can you believe it's the third anniversary of JFK's assassination?"

"I still can't believe he's dead," says Anne.

Debbie nods. "He was such an inspiration to this country."

Connie says, "Poor Jackie."

"The only reason Kennedy's a hero is because he was assassinated," Richard says, taking a roll and passing the basket to Connie. "He made a total mess of the Bay of Pigs. You know, just because he was good-looking doesn't mean he could run a country."

Henri brings in the turkey and sets it on the table. He sits down and looks around at his family. Ada recites, "Bless us, oh Lord, and these thy gifts…"

"Kennedy and his Camelot, what a damn joke," says Richard.

The tension around the table starts to increase. Ridley keeps looking at his father, who points to the food he wants passed to him. Debbie feels a headache coming on. Anne knows by the flutters in her stomach there's going to be another scene, just like there always is.

"So, how do you like Ridley's haircut, Ma?" Richard says. "He looks like a beetle—and I don't mean the band!" When he hits the table, everyone jumps as he laughs at his own joke. Ridley's face turns red. He looks at his father from underneath his bangs, and his expression is nasty. He wishes he could sneak outside and smoke some grass so he wouldn't care what his father said. One of these days, he knows his father will go too far and then—God help them both.

"Well. I think he looks like Paul McCartney," says Anne. "And he's *very* handsome."

"What the Christ do you know, pimple face?" Richard says loudly. Anne shrinks.

"What? You have your period?"

"Dad," says Debbie.

"It's true! Look at her."

Anne leaves the table crying. In the bathroom, she looks at her face in the mirror. She feels both shame and hatred that her father would embarrass her in front of everyone. What makes him so hurtful? Why does he drink and then become so mean?

"Richard. That was uncalled for," says Ada.

"She needs to toughen up," he says, finishing his drink. "The world is a mean place, and it will spit her out if she doesn't become harder."

Debbie studies her father. Is he really trying to protect her from the world outside? Did something happen to him when he was a kid? What in his past has driven him to such a toxic personality?

When it's time for dessert, Ada brings in an apple pie and a chocolate cream pie bathed in whipped cream.

"Where's the sharp cheese, Ma?" asks Richard.

Ada walks back into the kitchen and takes a deep breath.

Ridley yawns and says, "Excuse me."

"Are we boring you, Ridley?"

"No, Dad. I'm just tired."

"Yes, must be exhausting being a big football hero."

Anne returns to the table, red-eyed and sick to her stomach.

After the meal, Connie and Anne clean up. Connie puts her arm around Anne and whispers, "You're beautiful, sweetheart. We'll get some Clearasil. It's just a teenage thing."

* * *

The rest of the family sit in the living room as Richard starts harping on Deborah becoming a scientist instead of a physician.

"By the time she's finished, she'll have gone to school eight years to work in some dirty old lab. I don't get it."

Ridley says, "Scientists are very smart, Dad. You should be proud of her."

Richard rises from the couch. "I said to watch your tone with me." And then he tries to smack Ridley upside the head. But Ridley grabs his wrist hard and stops him dead.

"You think because you're a football star, you can talk to me like that?"

Ada says, "Richard!"

"Do not interfere, Ma. These are my kids, not yours. You did a bad enough job with me."

"I did my best."

"Right. Still have the paddle?" Richard says, sneering at his mother. "All you cared about was neatness and manners. What about affection, Ma? What about a little compassion? What about reading me a story every once in a while, uh?"

Henri remembers when Richard tried out for sports but didn't make any of the teams.

Debbie wonders if her father is actually jealous of Ridley.

Ada puts her head down. She never forgot the day Richard came home in '42 after trying to enlist in the army. He was classified 4-F, "unfit for military service," because of his eyesight. He was angry and ashamed of his rejection.

* * *

Richard gets up from the couch and goes into the kitchen, where he pours himself another double shot. Ridley has his face in his hands. Connie and Anne are finishing up in the kitchen and realize things are escalating. Anne's hands are shaking so badly she drops a glass on the floor.

"Jesus, Anne!" her father yells. "What the hell's wrong with you? Do you need glasses, too? Because your mother and I will certainly buy them for you," he says.

Ridley comes into the kitchen, gets a broom from the pantry, and starts sweeping up the glass.

But Richard grabs the broom and shoves Ridley aside. "Get the hell out of here."

Ridley's face is scarlet with rage. He gets in his father's face and says, "You know what? This is bullshit!" He walks down the hall to the spare room and lifts his jacket off the bed. Richard follows and grabs Ridley, pinning him against the wall and squeezing Ridley's cheeks hard with his right hand.

"You're not going anywhere. We leave when I say we leave. You hear me?"

Ridley forms a fist and is about to hit Richard when Henri walks into the room.

"Richard. Leave the boy be."

Richard starts yelling. "Mind your own damn business. Don't be acting the big man now when you never paid any attention to me as a kid. Where were you when I couldn't do anything right?"

"I said, leave the boy alone."

Richard lets Ridley go and leaves the room.

"You okay, Rid?"

"Now you see why I get high, Gramps?" Ridley rushes out of the room as Henri's shoulders sag.

Richard walks back down the hall and yells out, "Okay, party's over. Let's go, everyone!" He is overexcited, thanking his mother for the meal and shaking his father's hand. He helps Connie with her coat and smiles at everyone as if nothing has happened. The kids have their heads down as they assemble at the back door.

"Be careful on the stairs," says Ada, trying to keep from crying.

Connie lingers on the deck to talk to Ada and Henri, with her back to the stairs. Shaking her head, she says, "I'm so sorry. I don't know what gets into him."

The fact that Richard is an alcoholic is the elephant in the room.

* * *

Richard goes down the stairs first, swaying slightly. Ridley follows, carrying the bag of leftovers Ada has packed. Next comes Debbie.

Anne pauses on the deck and looks to the west at the setting sun. She stares at the red and gold streaks blazing across the November sky. The colors ignite a burning anger within her, and she knows the ranting will continue at home until her father passes out. That they will all pay for whatever went wrong today. She turns and looks at her family, who she loves deeply. But how much longer will they all have to suffer before the hurt and pain stops? She had never seen Ridley defend himself from her father until he tried to smack Ridley in the living room. What if Ridley decides to fight back someday? Then what happens? Surely, her father would be the one most hurt, but what if Ridley loses it and can't stop?

The family has just begun to descend the steps. Moving slowly with no conscious control of her movements, Anne walks across the deck and steps down behind Debbie. Her right-hand reaches out as she lays her hand on Debbie's back, who falls forward into Ridley, who tips into Richard, who topples down the stairs, bouncing off the railing and smacking the pavement below.

From the deck, Henri hears Deborah scream and sees what's happening. "Richard!"

Ridley has dropped the bag of leftovers, and a mason jar of cranberry preserves smashes on the stairs, smearing the steps in red chunks of splatter. Connie screams as the children surround Richard's still body.

"Oh my God," Connie cries, kneeling to put her hand on Richard's chest. Ada rushes into the house and calls an ambulance.

"Is he dead?" asks Anne, in a shaky voice, scared that she's responsible.

"I don't know," says Debbie, putting her arm around Anne. "Maybe."

Ridley stands transfixed, staring at his father's body. Only Anne and Deborah hear him whisper, "I hope so."

* * *

Richard is taken to Berkshire Memorial Hospital. Connie rides in the ambulance, and the rest of them follow in Henri's car.

In a small green hospital room with the curtain drawn, Richard lingers on life support for three days with a severe brain injury. His arm is in a cast, and his head is covered in a white bandage. There are tubes everywhere. A heart monitor beeps as if counting the minutes to his demise.

All of them struggle with their feelings of guilt and anger that their father was so hard to love, except for Connie, who remains by Richard's side weeping. On the third day, Richard quietly slips away, more at peace in death than he ever was in life.

Anne becomes hysterical, crying and sobbing. "It's my fault. I ran into Debbie, and then everyone fell into Dad! I killed him! I killed Daddy!" And then she runs to the bathroom and throws up.

No one believes Anne did it on purpose. The family tries to convince her it was an accident. But Anne remembers her hand on Debbie's back. Had she pushed her into Ridley, or had she just thought of doing it? Had Debbie been startled by Anne's hand on her back and fallen forward on her own? Debbie says she can't remember; it all happened so fast.

* * *

Anne's dreams haunt her until Debbie tells her and Ridley that they all need to see someone.

"I'm not going to a psychiatrist," says Ridley. "There's nothing wrong with me. The whole thing was an accident. I'm glad he's gone. End of story."

"That's just it, Ridley," says Debbie. "You're glad your father's dead. He was a mean-spirited alcoholic, and I think we all felt that way sometimes. In thought—if not—in deed. As a family, we can finally talk about it instead of hiding our hurt and anger."

"I'll go," says Anne. "I'm nauseous all the time from the nightmares and guilt. Maybe someone can help me with that."

"Ridley. I need help, too," says Debbie. "And I need all of you to be there so we can help each other."

Ridley frowns. "I guess you read a lot of cases about people's behavior, uh?" asks Ridley.

"Yes. But when it's personal, it's a lot different."

"What about Mom?"

"Mom turned a blind eye and probably understood Dad more than anyone else. We should definitely invite her to join us. But don't be surprised if she says going to church or the cemetery is all the help she needs. She knew he was an alcoholic, but she loved him unconditionally."

"Plus, he never hurt her," says Anne.

"I would have gone for him if he did," says Ridley.

Debbie and Anne remember how close Ridley came to hitting their father that dreadful Thanksgiving day. She did not want Ridley's anger, Anne's guilt, or her own inability to change her father to plague them for the rest of their lives. She knew they all needed to rid themselves of the baggage they would forever carry if they didn't get counseling now.

"So, we're agreed?"

Ridley and Anne nod, realizing their older sister is right.

Debbie pulls out a framed picture from her pocketbook of the three siblings standing in the water with the ocean behind them. At the time, they are sixteen, fourteen, and twelve. Ridley's arm is slung casually over Debbie's shoulder in a brotherly manner, while Debbie's arm is around his waist, pulling him in. Anne is leaning against Debbie, looking up at her with younger-sister adoration.

And their love for each other is as transparent as the water they stand in.

Scapegoat

"Thou know not all of what thou write," said a strange voice in the middle of the night.

It took me several seconds to awaken from the haze of a deep sleep. The room was cold and smelled of burnt wood, like a window was open and a fire had just gone out. I sat up in bed, peering across the room, and saw the shadow of a woman sitting in the chair. A slow, eerie tingling started in the middle of my back and spread across my shoulders. It ran down my arms and through my fingers like a wet hand on a light socket.

Who *are* you?" I whispered.

She sighed impatiently and said, "I am the one in thy book, and I cannot stay but a few hours to correct history."

I groped in the dark for the lamp switch. Squinting from its glare, my eyes traveled up and down her body taking in every detail as if I myself had dressed her and was checking for mistakes. Her hair was wild, thick, and black—like a forest with a face. She was wearing a red bodice laced up with red, green, and yellow strings and a white puffy blouse showing deep cleavage.

Her head tilted to one side, and her chin lifted as if challenging me to believe her.

"Dost thou know me now?"

I slowly nodded, unable to find my voice. Strange as it seemed, it had to be Bridget Bishop, the first woman hung for witchcraft in Salem, Massachusetts, and the protagonist in the novel I was writing. Or someone posing as her. But why? No one even knew I was writing again.

My mouth went dry. Was my obsession with Bridget's story making me hallucinate? I'd been writing from eight in the morning until eleven o'clock at night for the past year, and when I wasn't writing, she was constantly in my thoughts and in my dreams: when I cooked, when I showered, when I swept the floor. When I walked the grounds of my home.

Or —was it the abysmal loneliness of widowhood that had finally driven me batty? I closed my eyes and stuck my fingernail in the palm of my hand, pushing as hard as I could. But when I opened my eyes, she was still there.

Her legs were crossed, and her boot had a hole in the toe where a horrendous long, grey nail peeked out. I tried not to stare.

"Bloody frightful, is it not?" she said, holding her leg up. "I did once bite them off, but age came upon me, and me reach did fail me!" She slapped her thigh and cackled like a crow. I couldn't help but smile. She was exactly what I had envisioned, leaving me in a state of aching uncertainty.

* * *

In my early twenties, I first became fascinated with Bridget Bishop. It was Halloween in Salem, and as I walked down a cobblestone sidewalk, I heard shouting. Turning, I saw several men dressed in Puritan costumes chasing a woman. She, too, was dressed in costume but not the conservative dress of the Puritans. Her scarcely covered breasts bounced as she ran, and she held her skirt high over her boots. Frightened yet defiant, she yelled over her shoulder, "I am no witch! I am innocent!" I followed the actors toward Old Town Hall, where a mock trial was to be held. I learned that the woman being portrayed was Bridget Bishop, who would be hanged for nothing more than eccentricity and a failure to conform. That day, I witnessed only a snapshot of what had happened in 1692, but the scene haunted me like the sirens of the Gestapo in the film *The Diary of Anne Frank*.

After Bridget stopped laughing, I asked, "Why have you come here?"

"Dost thou not listen, writer? I am here to tell thee that which hath not been written afore."

"Why me? Why now?" I asked.

"No persons writ a book about me 'til now. I have waited three hundred years 'twixt heaven and earth to tell my story."

She was right, of course. The next day would be June 10, 1992. If this was a dream, it was the most vivid dream I'd ever had. "Would you like a cup of tea?" I asked, throwing off the covers.

"Indeed." She rose from the chair and sauntered out of the room like a queen leaving court.

* * *

When I got downstairs, she was staring out the kitchen window at the woods.

"How long hath thee lived in Andover?" she asked.

"Three years." I put the teapot on and set two cups on the table. "How do you take your tea?" I asked.

She turned and gave me an odd look. "With my hand."

"I mean, do you like milk and honey in your tea?"

"Well, why did thee not say that? And pray, what are those wee sacks in the cups? Art thou trying to poison me?"

"No, Bridget. They're called tea bags. It's how we drink tea now."

"Humph," she said. "A bit of milk will do. I have no need for honey. I am sweet as I am, think thee not?" she asked, smirking.

I grinned, but I doubt her sarcasm had amused the Puritans. Bridget jumped when the teapot whistled, and I lifted it quickly off the burner. After pouring the tea, I sat down to drink, watching her and pinching my thigh.

"So," I said. "What don't I know?"

"I am parched; hurry me not," she said, slurping her tea and imitating the way I lifted my pinky. "A fancy lady, eh?" she asked, placing the cup noisily in the saucer.

"Not really, but my mother was."

"Never knew me mum. She passed when I entered this world."

"In Norwich, right?"

"Aye."

"There's so little information about you."

"Why the devil dost thou think I have come?" she asked, looking at me like I was dense.

Hiding a smile, I grabbed a notebook and pencil from the counter.

Sitting down, I said, "Whenever you're ready."

"Dost thou know how it began?"

"Some of it. But I want to hear it from you."

* * *

"In those days, 'twas two Salem's. Salem Town—a busy port town with wealthy merchants, and Salem Village—where the poor farmers lived."

I nodded, remembering my frustration with the research on the borders between the two.

Amesbury, Andover, Beverly, and Rockport, an uninhabited section of Gloucester and Ipswich, were part of Salem Town then. Salem Village might have included Danvers, Marblehead, Salisbury, and Topsfield. But there is still much confusion as to where the lines were drawn even today.

'Twas Thomas Putnam's daughter, Ann, who danced in the moonlight with her friends and got found out. Said they were bewitched so they would get not in trouble. Put the blame on Sarah Good, a beggar woman, Sarah Osborne, an old wretch, and Tituba, a slave of Reverend Paris. Putnam was a great landowner in Salem Village. He and the elders brought forth charges against those poor women. Dost thee not think 'tis cowards who mark women of little means and odd temper?"

I nodded, feeling the anger rise.

"I lived in Salem Town, but they confused me with Sarah Bishop, a tavern keeper in Salem Village. I had not a tavern like they said, 'twas Sarah and Edward who owned the tavern."

"So, they got you and your second husband confused with Sarah and another Edward Bishop when they arrested you?"

She nodded. "'Twas four Edward Bishops at that time."

I snapped my fingers. "That's why you said at the trial that you never knew the people who accused you from Salem Village. You never lived there."

"I told them, *I never saw these persons before, nor I never was in this place before.* It helped not that I dressed with color and spoke my mind, and it mattered not if I was Sarah Bishop or Bridget Bishop. They had their scapegoat."

"Weren't you allowed counsel?"

"Counsel?"

"Someone who would speak for you in court?"

"I was naught but mud on their boots. Kept in jail for twenty-three days I was, in the most shameful of conditions, until they hanged me on June ten."

I wondered if her imprisonment reminded her of the meager rations she received because her next question came out of nowhere. "Dost thou have corn soup?"

"No, I don't. Would you like some breakfast?"

"I wouldst."

"I'll make you a frittata."

"Eh?"

"It's made with eggs and cheese, and mushrooms, peppers and onions. Then I bake it in a skillet."

"Aye. I shall eat that," she said, placing her cheek in her hand.

Bridget watched while I prepared our breakfast, sipping her tea and scratching her throat. I'd noticed a red welt around her neck in the morning light of the kitchen and felt a stab of compassion envelop me.

"Does your neck hurt?" I asked softly.

"Like a pox that wilt not leave my person."

I scooped the frittata onto a plate and offered it to her.

After breakfast, Bridget tried to help me clean up. She screamed when I sprayed the faucet hose around the sink.

"It's a bloody serpent!" she yelled, grabbing it from me as it squirted the window and counters. I took hold and put it back in its place.

"Bridget. It's only a hose," I said, laying my hand gently on her arm.

She held her head with her hands, eyes wide with fear. It struck me then that Bridget had confronted intimidation, humiliation, and hanging, yet a modern-day appliance had scared the bejesus out of her.

"Why don't you sit down, and I'll finish up."

She nodded and took a shaky breath. I stacked the dishes while she observed everything I did, her eyebrows furrowing as I pressed the button to start the dishwasher.

* * *

In my writing room at the back of the house, where long windows faced the fields and woods, I explained to Bridget how a computer worked. She sat in the chair beside me with her mouth open and eyes narrowed as the words she spoke appeared on the screen. "Saints in heaven," she said.

At one point, she sat back and waved her arm at the windows. "Dost thou own all this property?"

"Yes," I said. "My husband and I moved to Andover three years ago, but he died in a car accident." My heart raced at the thought of Connor.

"I was twice a widow," said Bridget. "I am sorry your husband passed, but you are fortunate to live in these times. Women owned naught in my day. We were nary more than farm animals. It mattered not that my second husband, Thomas, struck me on the Sabbath, and I struck back. We were gagged and tied for public misbehavior. Made us stand in the marketplace for hours, they did."

I shook my head and typed what she said.

"Samuel Wasselbee, my first husband, was a good man. I was but twenty years old when we wed at St. Mary-on-the-Marsh. Poor Samuel passed before we moved to Salem."

"So, you moved here by yourself."

She tossed her hair back. "I sought freedom in a new world. My charm and handsome countenance served me well, think ye not?"

Still typing, I said, "I think your beauty lies in your passion for life, Bridget. Which is part of what did you in."

"'Twas the times that did me in," she said. "That and a cunning twat named Mary Walcott."

Chuckling, I asked, "Did you use that word then?"

"Which word?"

"Twat."

"I cannot remember, bitch, twat, what matter of importance is it?"

I shrugged.

"The woman shouted in court that I bewitched her brother, that he tore my coat fighting off my specter. I had a tear in the same place he swore he tore it. They condemned me on spectral evidence, said my ghost bewitched him. What wouldst thou call her?"

I frowned as her eyes searched mine for the truth. Finally, I answered.

"Probably much worse."

Bridget laughed, and I picked up my manuscript, flipping to a page marked with a red tab.

"Can you tell me about the physical examination?"

"I wouldst rather birth in the public square than go through that again."

"What did they do?"

"Eight days afore my hanging, Sheriff Corwin ordered Rebecca Nurse, Alice Parker, Sarah Good, Elizabeth Proctor, and Susanna Martin to examine my person whilst I bent over. Said they found the teat of a witch betwixt my pudendum and my anus."

Groaning, I said, "Didn't they examine you a second time and say it was dry skin?"

"Aye."

I shook my head at their stupidity.

"They waited to hang me until after June eight, when the General Court passed a law saying witchcraft was punishable by hanging. Two days later, I swung from a tree on Gallows Hill."

"You never stood a chance," I said, shaking my head again.

"Nay. But who the devil were they to tell me how to live my life? Only my savior can do that."

"So, you believed in God?"

"Named my daughter Christian, did I not?"

"Yes, of course."

"I was the first to go," she said quietly. "They used me to scare the others."

"I know."

"Never did I think they would go that far."

About the others who had accused her: Ann Putnam, Abigail Williams, and Mercy Lewis, Bridget would only call them squawking hens. It was Mary Walcott and Cotton Mather, the minister who wrote the condemning pamphlets, who she blamed the most.

"I could have said I was a witch and been done with it. Deliverance Hobbs and Mary Warren did and saved themselves." Frowning, she added, "Deliverance went daft. I know not which is worse, hanging or being mad 'til you die."

"Why didn't you just confess?" I asked.

"Because I was no witch!" she said, holding her palms up like a petulant adolescent. *I am innocent as the child unborn,* I told Judge Hawthorne and that son of a pig, Jonathan Corwin."

"If you had it to do again, would you have given in and told them what they wanted to hear?"

She looked straight at me with red-rimmed eyes full of sorrow.

"I tell thee now that which I told them at the trial, *I know not what a witch is.* And then she added, "I would stay as God made me full of life and free as a crow."

I sighed. And not for the first time, I wished I could go back and change her fate.

Bridget had to go to the bathroom, and I showed her how to use the toilet and flush the chain. I heard her muttering, then laughing, flushing several times before she returned.

"I want to tell thee something else thou wilt get not from thy research," she said, adjusting her skirt.

"About the politics?"

"Nay—the fornication! I was always on top," she said proudly with her hands on her hips. "Rode my men like a horse!"

I laughed as she sat down.

"I remember the first time with Samuel," she continued. She stared at the woods with a faraway look on her face. "'Twas after the wedding at the inn. Thought I was afeard young bride. Got the surprise of his life he did.

Women in those days were hypocrites. "'Twas their duty," they said, whilst they primmed and pranced to the bedchamber. I pretended naught. Never was I false about anything in my life."

She daydreamed out the window while I typed.

"I took pleasure in the company of men," she said. "Held many a gathering at my home, and we had our share of cider."

"The cider got you into a bit of trouble, didn't it?"

"I made money is why. Sold it on the side and all, but they found me out. 'Twas when the first lies came about. They wanted a share of my profits, so they said I bewitched my husband, Thomas. I told them, *'If it please your worship, I know nothing of it'*. Wasn't for Reverend Hale, Pastor of the Church of Christ in Beverly, I would have gone to jail then. But as I was wont to do, I sought another way."

"How so?"

"I sold herbs."

"Herbs?"

"My grandmother schooled me in herbal medicine in Norwich. Even in her day, the growing of herbs wrought accusations of witchcraft. They said witchcraft passes down through the mother. 'Twas many a mother and daughter were accused or hanged. Sarah Good and her daughter, Dorcas, Ann Foster and her daughter, Mary, and Abigail Faulkner and *both* her daughters."

My eyes filled as I thought of all the innocent men, women, and young girls herded into jails or hanged because of fear and ignorance.

After a few moments I asked, "What kind of herbs?"

"Fennel for snakebites, marjoram for coughs, sage for fever, cilantro for stomach pain, and parsley root for the joints. And I grew jimson weed, which doth made thee forget all thy ailments!"

"Jimson weed?"

"Look not at me that way. Everyone hath thee spirits—though ye must be careful of the jimson weed. Give more than needed, and it wouldst take thee life. 'Twas called jimson weed for it began with early settlers in Jamestown, Virginia. They used it to ease pain 'til the villagers learnt it made them dream whilst they were awake!"

"You keep surprising me, Bridget," I said.

"Your third husband, Edward, never came to your defense at the final trial. Were you hurt by that?"

"I did not expect a coward like Edward Bishop ever would. If I hanged, he got the property bequeathed to me from Thomas. Edward thought they would accuse him too, so he shut his mouth, he did, and went along. The bastard wed again right after they hanged me."

"I'm so sorry, Bridget."

She looked at me, surprised. And then her eyes glistened. "No person ever said that to me afore." She bowed her head, and when she looked at me again, her face was wet with tears.

"Someone should have," I said, trying not to cry myself. I stood up. "Let's get some fresh air."

We sat on the Adirondack chairs facing the woods. The sky had turned a somber gray, and a warm breeze blew across the field. I wondered if it carried along the transgressions of the past.

"I noticed there were four Edward Bishops during the trials. Seems it was a very common name."

"Yes. Some were related, but not all."

Bridget grew quiet. I looked at her long, graceful nose, full mouth, and straight chin. Although she had the fair skin of the English, her fiery personality brought color to her cheeks as if they were sunburned. I could see why three men had wanted to marry her. But resiliency and stubbornness were also evident in her countenance.

"Thou art holding me memories in thy head?"

"Oh yes."

She turned and smiled. Her teeth were not bad for someone who'd probably never been to a dentist. She was swinging her foot, and I looked down at the ugly toenail protruding from her boot.

"Excuse me," I said and headed back in the house.

"Why dost thou leave?" she hollered.

"I'll be right back," I said. From the bathroom, I grabbed nail clippers and a bottle of bright red nail polish and hurried back outside.

"What the devil are those?" she asked with a scowl on her face.

"Nail clippers and polish for your toe," I said, kneeling down and untying her boots. Pressing down hard on the clippers, I said, "If it's going to peek out of your boot, then it might as well look pretty."

When I finished, Bridget clapped her hands and laughed. "'Tis the same color as me bodice!"

"Of course," I said. "I could also do your hair."

"How?"

"French braid it."

"I hate the French."

"They have nothing to do with it. It's what they call it, see?" I pulled my braid up into the air and showed her how it was intertwined. "It'll be fun," I said.

"Suit thyself," she said, but I could tell she was amused.

I went back inside the house and ran upstairs to the linen closet. I pulled out a brush, comb, elastics, and a mirror. I wondered when the last time was that Bridget had seen herself in a mirror. Then, I grabbed a jar of moisturizer and warmed a facecloth under the tap before I went back outside.

"Wert thee napping, dearest?"

"Sorry. I'm not as quick as you. Now sit still."

"Humph," was all she said.

For the next half hour, I French braided Bridget's hair, which nearly touched her waist. I gently washed her face and used the moisturizer to soften her skin. When I finished and stood back, I was not surprised at how attractive she was.

"Here. Look."

"They say a mirror wilt capture the soul of a dead person."

I could feel the goosebumps on the back of my neck. "Where did you hear that?" I asked.

"Thou must remember I am from a superstitious country. What was not understood—the plague or a bad harvest 'twas blamed on witchcraft.

"Ah."

"Hast thou lovers?"

"No," I said, wondering what made her think of that.

"Why not? Keeps thee youthful."

"I'm not ready."

"Thou mourn him still."

Barely above a whisper, I answered, "Every day."

She stared at me but said nothing.

"Did you ever have any female friends you could talk to? Someone that you trusted?" I asked.

"Most women cared not for me. They did not understand I was living my own life is all, in a land held fast by men."

"But didn't you realize, dressed like that, being outspoken, you were doing more than surviving?"

"I know not what thou mean," she said.

My voice had an edge to it. "Didn't you *know* that you were attracting attention and that it was the wrong kind of attention? Weren't you afraid of being rebellious? Afraid of death?"

"Indeed. Dost thee not think I liked being an outcast? I despised being in a jail with moldy food and dirty water. I was disgusted by the smell of me own waste a foot away from my person! They were trying to shame me, and I was damned if I would let them. I could not bear their hypocrisy."

I took a deep breath. "You were a feminist, Bridget."

"A what?"

"Someone who believes in equality for all women. Exactly what you were fighting for, although it didn't have a label then."

"A feminist, eh? Some good it did!"

I cringed, but she was laughing. I was amazed by her ability to rebound. I wanted her to stay forever, live in my world, and be my friend.

"I am hungry once more," she said.

"Can you stay for dinner?"

"I will," she said, but seemed unsure. "But I must bring something to the table. I shall come back."

She stood up and disappeared into the woods. I had no idea where she was going or when she would be back. I headed into the house and pulled a chicken out of the freezer. As I was peeling potatoes, she came in the back door carrying a hefty jug.

"What's that?" I asked.

"Cider."

"Where did you get it?"

"In good time, writer," she said, grunting, as she lifted the jug onto the counter. "Now take heed. Drink too much, and thou wilt land on thy buttocks!"

"Well, then, pour away," I said, looking out the window and wondering where in hell she got the jug. But I'd been transported to another plane of reality, accepting without question that she was the real thing. "Glasses are in the cupboard," I added.

* * *

"Tis it not unlike Thanksgiving," said Bridget, helping herself to the mashed potatoes. "Thou cook well. The chicken is tender, and thy gravy has much flavor."

"Thank you," I said. "Your cider's wonderful," I added, raising my glass for more. "I've never tasted anything like it."

"Nor will thee again," she said.

My expression changed. "Meaning?"

"I must leave soon. Afore I go, thou shall know something of utmost importance."

"I don't want you to leave," I said before thinking.

"Thou hath much work to do. Thou must finish thy book and tell the story the way it was."

"I know that," I said, unexpectedly filled with grief and longing. I was close to tears but kept on going. "I miss having someone to talk to. My husband was everything to me, and I didn't realize it would be so hard." Embarrassed, I looked away, blinking the dampness from my eyes. "I'm not strong like you.

I've always admired people who fight to the bitter end for what they believe in. I can only go so far, and then I always end up giving in."

"Women art strong, oft' times stronger than men. They bleed, they bear children, and they do the work of a man whilst they pretend the men are all-knowing. If thou were not strong, thou would care not for a large property, thou would rise not in the morning, dress, cook, or writ a book. Thou art moving on with life—it is not what it was, is all."

"Writing and sharing a life with my husband was all I ever needed."

To my surprise, I began to cry.

"Easy now. The cider has gone to thy head." She leaned over and put her hand on my shoulder. "Everyone needs a good cry. Thou art too afraid of showing what is inside."

"But I don't want to be weak!"

"Thou think crying makes thou weak?"

"Yes."

"Well, thou shall scream or holler if thou cannot cry. 'Twas what I did."

It was all I needed to hear from the woman I'd long admired for her bravery. Deep, heavy sobs erupted as I vomited my anguish. I cried for my husband, whose death I'd never fully mourned, too afraid of not being able to get back up if I broke down. I cried for Bridget, who'd been all alone in the fight of her life. And I cried for all the times I'd walked away instead of standing my ground, even if it meant standing alone.

After a while, my body stopped heaving. I took a cleansing breath and felt a sense of release and calm, as if I'd done something terribly wrong, then found out it wasn't my fault.

"Good. 'Tis time to make right the history. Fetch thy notebook."

* * *

I was back in seconds. She looked at me like a child hiding candy. I flipped to a clean page and snapped my pen.

"The rope was wrongly knot," she said, winking. "I had air enough to breathe."

"What are you saying?" I whispered.

"I lived."

My breath caught in my throat.

"My daughter, Christian, Sarah Lord Wilson of Andover, and a gravedigger named Caleb Butler came to my rescue."

"Sweet Jesus," I said as I wrote furiously, a euphoric sense of justice spreading through me.

"The villagers stayed not, ashamed of their silence. When the last person walked away, Christian, Sarah, and Caleb climbed to the platform and cut the noose. They wrapped me in blankets and put me in a wooden cart. Caleb threw dirt in the grave that he was told to dig for me dead body. We rode fast out of Salem through Salem Village to Andover."

I paused when Bridget said this.

"They took me to a cottage four miles into the woods on land called The Indian Ridge."

I looked up with an incredulous look. "Here?" I gasped. "Indian Ridge is right behind me!"

She nodded, smiling wide.

"Christian brought me back to health, and we lived out there," she said, pointing toward the woods, "Near a grove of apple trees. I stayed hidden and dressed in Puritan clothes, and I kept silent for once. Caleb brought supplies and sold my cider. No other persons ever knew what happened that day. Ten years later, I died from typhoid fever."

"Oh my God!"

I looked up and Bridget was watching my reaction. Then I jumped from my chair and threw my arms around her. "You won! You outsmarted the bastards! I can't believe it!"

I was laughing and crying at the same time.

"Believe it."

I sat down, turning page after page writing quickly and adding my notes in pure joy. When I started to say something, I looked up, but Bridget was gone. I ran to the back door and put on the floodlights, but there was no sign of her. I called her name again and again, but only silence responded. I felt abandoned, like a close friend had suddenly died. Hours later, as I lay in bed staring at the ceiling, I wondered if I would ever see her again.

* * *

The next morning, I woke early. All day, I'd hoped Bridget would appear. But she never did. It was dusk when I looked outside, drawn to the woods like a child to a forest in a fairy tale. And then I sprinted out the back door and across the field. For over an hour, I walked and ran, calling her name. My sneakers and jeans were splattered with mud, and I could hear the pounding of my feet as they hit the leaves and broken branches.

When I stopped and stood still, I was breathing heavily. It was quiet in the woods; not even a bird peeped. As sunset cast its magic spell through the trees. I turned around, smelling apples. Then, I saw the remnants of a partial fireplace. I moaned softly and leaned against a tree.

* * *

The flutter of wings caused me to look up at the darkening sky. Directly overhead, within a small patch of twilight, a large black crow paused in mid-air. I watched, confused by its stillness. And then, I began to feel an intense wave of awe and understanding.

I would stay as God made me, full of life and free as a crow," Bridget had said.

The crow hovered for a few more minutes. I stared, smiling, and then it flew away.

Jet Lag

It's two a.m., and Frank wants to fool around. In his world, it's three p.m. Beijing time, and he's ready for some afternoon delight. I hate to disappoint him, but I'm too tired to make love with the zest and creativity he'd like.

I slip out of bed and go to the bathroom, where the brilliance of a full moon illuminates the room. I linger at the window, hoping Frank will nod off. Staring up at the stars in awe of my own mini planetarium, I see Sirius, Orion, and planets whose names I've yet to learn. Whenever I feel like I'm drowning down here in the real world, the celestial world helps me rise back to the surface.

While Frank was in China, two planes crashed, and I immediately assumed they were terror attacks. I've always been superstitious: an empty chair rocking, an open umbrella in the house, a broken mirror, and, of course, bad things come in threes; myths taught by an Irish mother. Naturally, I thought there was one more crash to go and worked myself into a small frenzy. Even now, I feel the residue of stress, though he's home safe.

Frank is still awake when I shuffle back to our room. He's a weary but randy traveler. A heavy arm curves around my waist, and he begins nuzzling my neck.

"Frank, honey, I'm beat. Maybe tomorrow night?"

He pulls back immediately. "Sorry. I'll go downstairs."

I feel bad, so I say, "That's alright, stay," but I don't mean it. From experience, I know he'll toss and turn all night and make those creepy jungle noises.

"I'm only going to keep you up," he says, getting out of bed. "I'll come back later."

I lie there and listen as he goes down the stairs. The third step squeaks from his weight, and I follow him in my head as he closes the French doors to the living room and the panes rattle in a hundred-year-old house. He'll watch recordings of the Discovery channel or NOVA, then come back up and sleep until noon.

Before Frank got home, I'd lain awake trying to plan for a future without him if his plane did crash. I figured if I prepared for the worst scenario, anything less would be a bonus.

First, I'd have a garage sale. My friend, Abby, would help because she's always trying to get rid of things. Then I'd sell the house because it's too big to take care of alone. I'd stay in town where I have friends and a good hairdresser. Then I'd move to a condo in one of those reconverted mansions on Parker Road, although I probably wouldn't have a garage and have to scrape the snow off in winter. So maybe I'd get a condo closer to the ocean with an attached garage. I can make it alone. I'm strong. Maybe stronger than I think. Maybe I'm so strong I shouldn't even worry about being strong.

And then I realize I'm kidding myself. Losing Frank would kill me. So, I make a deal with my Maker. I'll go to church more than just once on Christmas. I won't keep the free cards and return address stickies unless I actually donate to a cause. I'll cook every day of the week. Except on Saturdays, and maybe Wednesdays or Thursdays, either one or maybe both.

Adding to my stress is the loss of my mother three months ago. Frank told me once that my resiliency is my greatest strength. This surprised me because I never thought of myself in that way. I suppose because my internal thoughts aren't visible, I look tougher than I am. Carrying the grief of my mother's passing is like a suitcase in my stomach, and I'm afraid that once I open it, everything inside will spill out. I adored my mother. She was sweet and kind and good to me when she wasn't being surly, and before she didn't know me anymore. But it's important that I hold it together as I'm also running the wedding of our daughter, Melanie, who's getting married in three weeks. Worst part is— I don't even like my daughter.

They say God only gives you only what you can handle but I'm not sure of that anymore. And, if it is true, why isn't he letting me sleep so I can handle all this stress? I can't remember the last time I slept for more than two hours at a time.

After Frank got in last night, he wanted to watch television so he could unwind. "Sure," I said. *Real Time* with Bill Maher was on, but five minutes after the monologue, Frank was sound asleep in the recliner, head back, mouth open, and snoring like a symphony of wildlife.

"Frank," I said. "Let's go to bed." The recliner sprang to life like a jack in the box.

"I'm good. Just resting my eyes."

"Do you want something to eat?"

"What, hon?"

"Want something to eat?"

"Oh good."

"Oh good, what?"

"You turned up the heat."

"That's not what I said, Frank. I said do you want something to eat?"

"Oh. Sorry. Sure. I'll do it."

Making something to eat will prove to me he was only dozing and now he's ready to fight the world and cook a bagel. He's good for another twenty minutes after he's eaten, and then, sure enough, I heard the din of a wildebeest.

I made a racket when I picked up his empty plate, stomped to the kitchen, bumped the plates in the dishwasher, and, as a last resort, sang at the top of my lungs, "Ain't no sunshine when heee's gone." Nothing. I walked back to the living room.

"Frank."

"Okay." He rose from the recliner, yanked up his pants, and headed upstairs. Following him, I saw the drag in his carriage from a thirteen-hour plane ride. It saddened me that he had to travel so much because business was down. As Director of Operations for a semiconductor company, Frank's business was going through a major downturn, and he's overseas much more than normal. The cost of Melanie's wedding has put additional pressure on both of us. Especially since I quit my job as a copy editor at *The Paramount Review* because I wanted to be with my mother during her last months.

Melanie moved to Palo Alto last year to head up the Marketing Division of a start-up company. She wanted to be married here in Massachusetts, so I'm left with all the arrangements, including the fitting for her wedding gown. I resent this responsibility, but because I feel guilty about my lack of maternal love for my own daughter, I compensate by overcompensating.

"Mother," she instructed me yesterday in her Miss Corporate America tone. "You're the exact same size as me, just make sure the length is right with the two-inch heels in my shoe rack. Not the gray open-toed shoes, the tan Ferragamo's with the strap around the ankle. Have you started the place cards yet?"

I took calligraphy classes a few years ago so now she wants the cards hand-written with a fountain pen. The wedding is less than three weeks away, and no, I haven't started the place cards yet.

* * *

Two days later, Melanie's up and at it, calling to follow up on our last conversation. "Mom. Did you go for the fitting? The tiara should be at home on my bureau wrapped in tissue paper."

The tiara. Of course. No traditional veil for Melanie, her Royal Highness Princess of Nothingham. Does she even think of my mother, her grand-mother, or realize she won't be at the wedding?

"Yes. I went for the fitting this morning. It was fine. I brought the dress home, and it's hanging in your room." I want to add that Seamus, our Main Coon cat, clawed the lace at the hem so badly that I had to cut a huge chunk off. But I know she won't appreciate the levity.

"Okay, gotta run. Make sure you order the flowers. Remember, the blue and purple hydrangeas, not the pink, and not that regular blue you see everywhere."

"Will do." I hang up the phone as gently as possible lest I smash it against the wall.

* * *

Frank's been working from home since he got back and told me this morning that the tide is turning. "Really, hon," he said, "The—tide—is—turning." He's been awake since four o'clock, meaning I've been awake since four o'clock. I measure four tablespoons of Ethiopian dark roast coffee to one cup of water, realizing its time to make a change and sleep in the guest room.

"Frank. Let's go for a walk this afternoon so you can get more daylight. It will help you sleep better." Frank is scratching his stomach while looking out the kitchen window at the birdfeeder.

"Wow, need to feed the birds already."

"You were gone for a week and a half, Frank. They go through that feeder in two days. You need to get a larger container that meters out the birdseed because I'm tired of hauling it out to the garage, filling it, lugging it back, then swinging it onto the hook while teetering on a warped piece of pavement left over from the previous owners. It's a balancing act, Frank. If I didn't enjoy watching the birds so much, I'd swing it out into the woods."

Frank stops scratching. "Let's go for a walk."

* * *

We stroll through the garden cemetery, up and down hills, past the ornate mausoleums, and around the pond. It's a beautiful September day, and the leaves are just starting to turn. But I'm so tired. I feel like my body is made of heavy metal. As I slog along the walkways, I look at the gravestones and envy the sleep of the dead. Frank doesn't notice I'm lagging behind and remarks on how many monuments have Armenian names.

That night, Frank stays awake until eight o'clock before passing out in the recliner. I rouse him at nine and tell him I need to sleep in the guest room. But I can hear the bed springs through the wall from his body bouncing, and he's making zoo babble again. I go to the bathroom window and stare at the stars, wondering if there's other life up there and how I can afford a shuttle to the moon.

On the way back to bed, I pass Melanie's wedding dress hanging on her door, reminding me of how much I still have to do and how apathetic I feel about it. Then, I feel guilty for feeling apathetic. Then I wonder if the third crash will be Melanie's plane on the way home for the wedding—punishment for not loving my daughter the way a good mother should.

Just as I'm finally nodding off, I hear the phone ring downstairs. I'd shut it off in our bedroom so it wouldn't wake Frank. Mel is crying so hard I can't understand a word. Apparently, she'd had an argument with Seth, her fiancé, who was getting cold feet.

"What the hell am I supposed to do? The wedding is three weeks away!"

I feel like my major organs are on an elevator, plummeting to the basement.

"What exactly did he say?" I ask with forced kindness.

"He told me he loves me, but the huge ceremony and promises for forever are scaring the shit out of him."

"Oh dear. You think he's going to call it off?"

"I don't know!" she yelled. I took a deep breath and, mustering all the patience I could, I asked, "When do you think you'll know, sweetheart?"

Click.

"Melanie?"

* * *

I don't tell Frank about Melanie. Since business is not good and he's 65, ten years older than me, and overweight, I think heart attack or stroke. The responses are still coming in, and we're up to one hundred and eighty-nine guests.

It's three in the afternoon, and I should start the place cards, but I have no desire to do anything. Besides which, I'm afraid I'll smudge the ink. I'm so jittery. I haven't done the breakfast dishes yet, and Seamus's hair is in fur balls in the corners of rooms, in soft clumps on the carpets, and on my clothes, because I haven't brushed him, and his hair floats in the air. I know because I was sitting in the dining room yesterday just watching it floating in a ray of sunshine. Furry little particles in white, grey, and brown, like they're part of the air. Hair air. Everywhere.

Then, while putting away Frank's suitcase, a lovely little bottle of Ambien rolled out of the side pocket. I don't like taking drugs, but surely this was a sign from above. I take two, and that night, for the first time in years, I get five hours of sleep without waking up.

There's no word from Melanie, however, and the wedding is now fourteen days away. Trepidation follows me like a ghost, grief has a tight hold on my chest, and the threat of a third crash still looms. But when? Who? I double the Ambien because all I want to do is escape or fly out the bathroom window and sit on the Big Dipper.

Frank still hasn't filled the birdfeeder yet, and I miss hearing their chatter. But I'll be damned if I'm going to fill it even though they'll probably end up lying flat on their backs, feet up, and stone dead from starvation.

* * *

When Frank got up this morning, he asked why I made cupcakes with Dijon mustard frosting and tiny marshmallows on top. I think for a long time why I would do something like that, but I can't come up with an answer.

"You okay, Liz? You look a little flushed."

"Yes, because I'm making blueberry pancakes." He's not aware of my promise to God to cook more often.

Maybe Frank had dreamed it, a side effect of his jet lag. I run to the wastebasket and see half a dozen broken cupcakes with burnt mustard and little marshmallows on top. Oh God. What if I have early-onset Alzheimer's? I've been afraid of that since my mother died, and I found out it could be hereditary. She'd been a little quirky, my mom, like buying those squeaking frogs and placing them on each stair so when you walked up, they croaked, "Ribbet, ribbet."

Visions of my mother's blank stare at the end and the food stains on her hospital gown stagger me for a moment. I shut my eyes tightly, willing myself not to break down. Then I feel another stab of heartache when I realize I will never have the relationship with my daughter that I had with my mother.

* * *

Frank said I was slurring my words this morning, but I think it's because I'm still drowsy from another night of delicious sleep. It's like the peaceful trance I feel when stargazing from the bathroom window. He doesn't know I renewed his prescription and I could probably sleep through an alien invasion. Sometime during the night, I supposedly ran into the bedroom and asked him what was on the guest room ceiling, insisting there was a big green bug with little babies following behind. Frank got up and checked and said there was absolutely nothing there.

The movie *Gaslight* comes to mind. But why would Frank try to make me think I was going crazy? He loves me. Everyone says so. But does he really? What about poor Abby, who'd been completely blindsided when her husband asked for a divorce? Turned out he was in love with a twenty-two-year-old from Taiwan.

Maybe Frank met someone in Beijing, someone with long black silky hair and porcelain skin with no sun damage. I remember a *Law & Order* episode where the defense attorney accused Detective Lupo of yellow fever, referring to men who preferred Asian women. Had that happened to Frank? Is that why he's been going to China more lately?

Melanie called today all sweet and cheery to tell me the wedding's back on. She's really getting on my nerves with this diva stuff. I have no illusions of happily ever after with either of them, but I said a silent prayer of thanks to God, then asked for another favor.

"Please don't let their flight home be the third crash even though I suck as a mother."

* * *

I vaguely remember the siren, but didn't think it was for me even though I'd crashed into a mailbox on Wood Hill Road.

All cops seem tall to me, especially when you're sitting in your car, and they're standing like a giant beside your window in full uniform, wearing a gun and looking officious.

"License and registration, ma'am."

I pull it from the glove box and hand it over. The next thing I know I'm home, sitting in my kitchen while a cop explains to Frank what happened. Turns out Frank and the cop, whose name is Mac, know each other from the Elks Lodge.

"She was driving ten miles an hour without her lights on, Frank, and still took out a mailbox."

I sit there staring at the two men as if I'm half asleep.

"Have you been drinking, ma'am?"

I try to focus on every word because they all seem like loose puzzle pieces in my head. "I never drink and drive."

"Are you on any medication that would make you drowsy or unable to function normally?" he asks.

"Um," I say, looking thoughtful. My face feels hot, and I'm starting to sweat. Suddenly, I realized that the third crash I'd been so afraid of was not Frank's or Melanie's plane at all. It was *my car* that crashed! A huge smile of relief spreads across my face. Frank and Mac look at me like I've truly lost it.

"Something funny?" asks Mac.

"I'm sorry. I'm very tired and feeling a bit giddy." I had to come clean sooner or later, but I didn't want to admit that I'd not only stolen Frank's Ambien, I'd also renewed his prescription behind his back.

I look at Frank. He looks at me. Mac has his hands folded over his belly. Frank offers him coffee as I sit there, contemplating my strategy.

"Mrs. Randolph? Did you hear my question? Are you on any kind of medication that would make you drowsy or unaware of your surroundings?"

"Give me a sec. I'm going through my list of pills."

"You take a lot of them?"

"No, mostly vitamins. Let me think now if I've taken anything new."

I look up at the ceiling, squinting.

"I may have taken some of Frank's Ambien." I'm hoping that involving an upstanding Elk like Frank will make Mac go easier on me. After all, I'd just run into a dumb mailbox. Frank nods and puts his arm around me.

"That explains it. I've been traveling a lot lately, and it takes me a while to resume a normal sleeping pattern. My doctor prescribed Ambien to get me back on schedule." Frank gets up to pour Mac's coffee.

"Liz, are there any scones left?"

"I'm good, Frank, coffee's fine." Mac takes a healthy gulp, slurping a little. I know it's delicious, because Frank makes the best coffee in the world. Mac doesn't say anything for a while, and we all just sit there. The only thing that's keeping me conscious is worrying about what he'll decide.

Finally, pointing at me, Mac says, "Look. Knock off the Ambien, you understand? I think you're one of those people that's had a severe reaction. We've had a few cases, so I'm familiar with the symptoms. And Frank," he says pointing to him, "You need to keep those pills away from your wife and be careful yourself." He rises from the chair and says, "By the way, I had her car towed to Buzzy's. Thanks for the coffee—good stuff."

After Frank closes the door, I stand against the wall in the kitchen, waiting for his reaction, my heart pounding like a battle drum.

"Are you out of your mind? You could have killed yourself! Do you realize that? What if some drunk had rear-ended you while you're in la-la land driving down Wood Hill Road?" Frank's temples are pulsing and some of his spittle lands on my cheek. I have never seen him like this before, and I want to make a run for it.

"I'm sorry." The room is starting to spin.

"You've been taking them since I got back, haven't you?"

"Sort of." Frank's voice sounds far away.

"And you renewed the script."

I nod slowly. "I…just…needed…some…sleep." I look at his fuming face and, to my horror, slide down the wall to the floor like a razed building, crumbling slowly to the ground in a cloud of dust. This is followed by an outburst of sobbing, which becomes uncontrollable, as if every ounce of water in my body is coming out of my eyes and nose, flooding my face. Frank walks to the kitchen window spreading his arms across the counter with his back to me.

Finally, he turns around, a look of compassion on his face. "What the hell's going on, Liz?"

I try to calm down. I wipe the snot from my nose with the back of my hand and start rocking back and forth, holding on to myself like I'm in a padded cell. Frank stands there baffled. After a long while, I start to talk in a low voice.

"I just couldn't handle it anymore."

"Handle what?"

Frank sits down on the floor beside me and reaches for my hand. "Talk to me, Liz."

"Everything. First the two plane crashes and worrying that yours would be the third. My mother's death, the wake, the funeral. Running a wedding for that spoiled brat, we call our daughter and Seth about to call it off."

Frank is looking at me like he's just discovered I have green eyes.

* * *

Melanie and Seth arrive the day before the wedding. I'd finished the place cards the morning after my meltdown. It took over six hours and I kept stretching my cramped hand when I finished. When I went downstairs, they were all having breakfast.

"Good morning, everyone! Today's the big day!"

"Yeah. Except for these," said Melanie, picking up four place cards and pushing them towards me on the table.

"You need to correct these cards, mother. They're misspelled, and some of the ink has gone sideways."

I closed my eyes.

"Melanie," said Frank. "They'll just have to do. There's no time for her to correct them before the ceremony."

"No way!" she yelled. "She had plenty of time to do it right!"

"Calm down," I said. "I'll finish them. But just once, Melanie, I'd like to hear you say, 'Thank you, Mom. I really appreciate all that you've done for me.'"

"Oh, for God's sake, can't you see how stressed I am?"

* * *

I finished the cards and climbed the stairs, carefully removing Melanie's gown from its hanger. It was a beautiful dress. Then I thought of how self-absorbed she'd become, treating me like her maid, lacking any compassion for my grief, and showing absolutely no appreciation for all I'd done for her.

Very gently, I turned the wedding gown over. The small cloth buttons that ran down the back of the dress were all fastened. Starting with the third button down, I snipped off four of the buttons in a row with a pair of manicure scissors, leaving a wide gap where Melanie's large purple birthmark would show. I would be helping her dress, and she'd never notice until it was too late.

I told myself it was so she could get some air amid all that lace and tulle. But it might have been the Ambien still in my system…

The Ballad of Henry Withers

He looks like Jesus in jeans, sitting on a stool with a guitar tilted on his thigh. His slender fingers pluck the strings, and his brown hair falls softly to his shoulders. He is eye candy in its purest form. When he looks up, his soulful eyes search the crowd and find hers. She stares back, letting him know she is there. But it becomes awkward, so she looks away.

They'd met four years ago. He was just starting out and only sang a few songs along with two other bands. But his were by far the best. His range of voice was perfection, moving effortlessly from low to high pitches.

But it was his lyrics that attracted her most. He sang of kings and paupers, God and creation, midnight dreams, and desire. To her, he was a poet, and she hoped he was as deep as his words.

Afterward, he asked her to dance, but others slyly cut in, and he moved away and let them.

She wasn't sure if he was being polite or enjoying the attention. Rugged and good-looking, she wondered if he was the bad boy women couldn't resist. And was afraid she was one of them.

Twenty-one at the time, she fell hard. She'd had a few lovers before him, immature boys who just wanted a roll in the hay and weren't very good at it. But he was older and more confident with the swagger other guys only dreamed of. They started dating and he'd waited for her to take it to the next step. She liked that about him. When it finally happened, she was more than ready. They stayed at a cabin in the woods, and when she woke up, she heard the birds chirp and smelled the earthy scent of nature. She could tell he cared for her by the way he'd made love to her—slowly, gently.

"Did you sleep okay, Lily?" he asked, leaning on his elbow. With the back of his hand, he stroked her cheek. She looked up, huddled in the sheets and quilt, so relaxed all she could say was, "mmm."

"You remind me of a baby bird swaddled in its mother's nest," he said. She smiled, feeling her whole body soften with his words.

She started following him on the road whenever she could, forming friendships with band members' girlfriends, especially Tommy Colton's girl, Annie. They slept at the same motels and ate at the same diners.

* * *

Tonight, they're at the same barn where they met, and his stage presence is impressive. Is it his success that's made him seem bigger than life? She thinks yes.

"Thank ya'll for comin' out on such a nasty night, Missoula," he yells out to the audience, his voice a blend of cream and gravel. Shouts of support and high-clapping hands follow as the spotlight focuses on the stage. His eyes squint but he finds her once more and grins as if all is forgotten. She's angry at herself because he still has the ability to unnerve her. Just because she's shown up at his show doesn't mean she's forgiven him for the pain he has caused her.

When the clapping slowly dwindles, the crowd watches him with wet, stringy hair and adoring faces that glisten from the sleet outside. Lightening flashes through the high windows of the barn, and the audience roars and stamps their feet on the sawdust floor. He smiles, waiting for silence to descend. When it does, Snake and the River Rats make everyone forget the thirty-five-degree temperatures and freezing rain outside.

She sways to the music, high from the weed Tommy Colton and she shared on the porch before the show. When he'd offered it, she'd taken a hit, hoping it would calm her down.

Snake is strutting across the floor, shifting his guitar up and down and then he kneels, throwing his head back. The fans scream, holding their phones in the air for photos. Toward the end of the first set, he stops and changes guitars, his hair, and T-shirt soaked with sweat.

"This here's a ballad I wrote during my young and reckless days," he says. A hush comes over the audience as they sense a change in his mood. He looks out at the crowd and strums a few notes. They wait, anticipating the next song. "A'right. Here we go."

Henry Withers was a fool, as Silver Creek knew well,
He threw away his lady for a sassy wench from hell,
Henry Withers is alone now, and the wench she married not,
And the lady Henry loved? Well, she married William Brock.
Henry Withers, Henry Withers, how could you still want more?
Your lady friend was lovely, and your sassy wench, a whore.
Your ego got the best of you, took you down, and laid you bare,
And now there's just the music and a heart you can't repair.

Seven hundred voices join the chorus as the song relates the tale of a lost fool. There's a deep longing in his voice, and the melody is beautifully bittersweet. Lily's heart is stirring, surprised at his public display of recklessness. Yet, she is guarded because of his betrayal.

It is hard to stop the crowd from yelling, "Bravo! You rock it, Snake! We love you!" And he responds, "I love you, too, Missoula! Don't go away. We'll be back!"

* * *

Band members and fans stand at the bar talking, guzzling beer, and downing shots. She is standing back and sees him surrounded by nubile women, showing perky cleavage, craving an autograph, and most likely more. Each time he takes a swig, he turns, his intense brown eyes roaming around the room over the top of his beer. Then he stops when he sees her. No smile, no, 'come on over,' just a steady stare.

She walks to the bar, squeezing between two beefy guys who reek of booze and body odor. She is petite and waving for service gets pushed aside. Then she feels an arm rise over her head. The bartender immediately comes over. "Another Bud, Snake?"

"Not for me, Pete. For the lady here." She recognizes the dulcet voice of the band leader.

Play it cool; it's only a beer. "Thank you," she says, looking up at him.

"You're welcome," he says and bends in a bow.

She can't help but smile. "Nice ballad."

"Thanks for coming, Lily. It's wonderful to see you."

"I'm curious. How many people know *you're* Henry Withers?"

"Doesn't matter. You're the one I wanted to hear it."

"Is that why I got a personal invitation and a free ticket?"

He nods and stares again. "Part of my penance."

"Really. They're just lyrics. It doesn't mean you won't do it again."

"Biggest mistake of my life." Then he stares at her again, taking her in from head to toe.

"What's with the staring? You got something to say?"

"Yeah. You're lookin' *real* fine, Lily."

"Finer than Jess Watkins?"

He closes his eyes. She takes a swig of beer.

"Lily," he says softly, "Please. You gotta give me another chance."

She looks into his eyes, and it's hard not to believe he's sincere. He was always a gentleman in a world where the f-word had become common, and men often forgot how to treat a lady.

"You know the old saying, Henry, 'Once burnt twice shy.'"

"I do know. But I've learnt my lesson. I swear on my ma's grave."

She shakes her head and looks away.

"Lily." The way he says her name is like a caress, and she feels its effect. "You know I wrote that song for you. I wanted to go up on that stage in front of everyone and admit what an ass I was."

"You sure were, cowboy."

Doesn't that tell you *something?*'"

"Like I said, it doesn't mean you won't do it again."

"You're not going to make it easy for me, are you?"

"Hell no. Why should I?"

He takes a deep breath.

"Change the subject, *Snake*." He winces at her sarcastic pronunciation of his stage name.

"Tommy tells me you won the Big Sky Sharpshooter Award this year."

"Yep."

"Congratulations. Heard you're giving riding lessons again at December Ranch."

"Have you been keeping tabs on me?"

"Yeah. Tommy gives me all the news. What else you been doing with yourself?"

"Well, I've got twenty-five students now, and I board Sugarbaby and three other horses at the ranch. I've been training Sugar, and thinking of showing her. She's still young, and she jumps high and clear."

"She's a great horse."

He was always great with Sugar, talking in soft tones to her, patting the sides of her neck and stomach, brushing her down after every ride. Sugar responded in kind to his calm and tender touch, snorting and shaking her head up and down whenever he approached her stall.

"That she is."

Looking at her left hand, he says, "Where's your ring?"

"Pawned it and bought a new saddle for Sugar."

"Didn't work out?"

She hesitates. "Some things got in the way."

"Some*things* or some*one*?"

"Not your problem."

"Yeah, it is. I love you, Lily."

Tommy Colton suddenly nudges in and tells Snake it's almost time. "Hey, Lily. How you doin'?"

"Good, Tommy. Thanks." The weed has mellowed her, but she is still riddled with mixed emotions, trying hard to tamp them down.

"How about you?"

"I'm rockin' it. Just trying to keep my friend here in line."

"Must be a full-time job. Where's Annie? I was hoping to run into her."

"She's got a massive cold, and she's full of NyQuil, day and night," he says, laughing.

"Please tell her I hope she's feeling better—and I miss her."

Tommy nods. "Will do, Lily."

Two other band members begin walking toward the stage. Henry bends down and whispers, "C'mon Lily. I've changed. Let me prove it to you. You'll see."

"Right."

"Look," he says. And there it is—the tattoo of a red lily on his upper arm. She shrugs. "They say those things hurt like hell when removed."

"That's not why it's still there."

She tries to pretend she doesn't care. But she does.

* * *

She thinks back to when he first got the tattoo. They'd driven up to Butte in her truck, and she thought their relationship would be as permanent as the ink on his arm. He wore sleeveless T-shirts from then on to show it off. When he became more popular, women started grabbing for him, touching him, asking for autographs, and inviting him to parties. It had been so good for so long until she found out he slept with Jess Watkins. Thank God, she'd always made him wear protection. Later, she asked herself if she had suspected he might cheat—or had she just been smart?

After she left him, he called day and night, came to the ranch, begging for her to forgive him. But she was too hurt. He sent her flowers and told her about the song he was writing and dedicating to her. Tommy came over and told her that Henry had canceled two of his gigs, he was so upset about the breakup.

"He's not right, Lily. He's drinking a lot, then he talks about you, but no one can understand him in his drunken stupor. I swear to you, he hasn't even looked at another woman, and believe me, they're all over him like bees on honey. Can't you just give him *some* hope?"

That was almost a year ago, and when she got the invitation to the concert in Missoula, she decided to go and test her feelings, convince herself it was truly over. As soon as he sang the ballad, she knew how easy it would be to fall in love with him all over again.

* * *

"Why didn't you answer any of my calls?"

"There was no reason to."

He puts his hand on her back and guides her to a quieter corner. Tommy is waving to him to get going.

"Can't we even talk about this? I screwed up, Lily. I'll do anything you say, just come back to me. It was a stupid fling with Jess and didn't mean squat. And it cost me the one person who meant more to me than anyone else in the world."

She'd never seen him so vulnerable. This was not the same guy she'd slapped across the face and told to go to hell when she'd first confronted him. Who'd thought it wasn't that bad because he was drunk? Until she left him and he realized how wrong he'd been.

* * *

Lily leaves after the second set. He calls her the next day and asks her to lunch at Jeffrey's Tavern. She's interested in what else he can say that will change things. But she'd noticed the night before that he paid no attention to any of the women clawing at him, and he signed no autographs. It was all about her.

He waves to her from the window seat that overlooks Blackfoot River. She's wearing jeans, a white turtle-neck sweater underneath a down jacket, and high leather boots. Her hair is in a ponytail, and her cheeks are red from the cold wind. Henry stands up and gives her a hug before she sits down.

"I ordered you a Bud, if that's okay?"

"Yes, that's okay, Henry," she says, smiling at his manners.

He leans forward and tents his fingers on the wood table. "Thanks for meeting me. I was so happy you came last night." He doesn't mention that she left early or that nothing had been resolved between them.

"I left because I was worried about the weather driving home."

"Of course. I figured that."

She picks up the menu, blocking him from view while she reads the choices. Then she puts it down and looks out the window. The freezing rain the night before left the Blackfoot River frozen on each side as the center of the river winds its way around the mountains. Since the release of the movie, *A River Runs Through It* with Brad Pitt, the Blackfoot River has become much more famous for its fly fishing and countless rapids. Lily remembers many good times there, especially when she and Henry floated down the river on inner tubes, laughing so hard they tipped into the river.

"You remember…"

"I do," she cuts in. "I remember a lot of things, Henry. That's why it hurt so bad when you threw it all away."

"I know, Lily. I wish to hell I could take it all back. But I can't, and I have to live with what I did."

She knows he's hurting, and it's hard to watch. "What are you having?" she asks.

"Um, I guess the bison burger. What about you?"

"Sounds good."

There's an awkward silence between them, and then she hears him sigh, knowing something's coming. Then he reaches into his pocket, pulls out a tiny velvet box, and puts it in the center of the table.

"God damn it, Henry! What the hell is this? It's too soon—waaay too soon."

"I know. I know it is. And it doesn't mean we're engaged. I just want you to know how serious I am about starting over. Not until I lost you did I realize how much you meant to me. I want you forever, Lily. You don't have to wear the ring. I just saw it, and it reminded me so much of you I had to buy it. Keep it in a drawer if you want, or keep it anywhere you want. I just want you to have it."

She stares at the box. "How long have you had this?"

He looks embarrassed. "Three months. After I came out of my shell of shame, I saw it in a jewelry store in Billings. It was so beautiful; it reminded me of you. Don't you want to look at it?"

"No. Not now." She picked it up and put it in her pocketbook. "Can you return it if I decide I don't want it?"

His shoulders slump. "Yeah, sure."

* * *

The box sits on Lily's kitchen table for three days before she opens it. When she does, she sees the large diamond surrounded by emeralds in the shape of lilies. It must have cost him a small fortune, and she doubts there are many like it. She tried it on, and to her surprise, it fit perfectly. And then she put it back in the box.

For nearly a week, she doesn't take Henry's calls as she weighs the pros and cons of reuniting. She rides Sugarbaby out past the ranch, stopping at an overlook and thinking about a future with—and without Henry. Can she survive another break up, and is he worth the risk to try again?

"What do you think, Sugar?" Sugarbaby snorts and turns her neck. "Is that a yes?" She snorts again and bounces her head up and down. Lily rides across the ridge and doesn't go back to the ranch until dusk. She gets off the horse and walks him for a few miles until the sun is almost setting.

When she returns, she calls him.

* * *

They walk along the L trail on a sunny Saturday afternoon. He makes her dinner that night and sets the table with a lit candle. Broiled whitefish, scalloped potatoes with cheese and onion, and winter squash are prepared with fresh herbs and served on nice platters and porcelain bowls.

"You didn't have to do all this, Henry, but where in the heck did you learn to cook like this?"

"Honestly? I had visions of doing this if I ever got the chance again. I bought some cookbooks and thumbed through them until I found one I thought I could do."

"Where did you get these lovely dishes?"

"Online from the Le Creuset website," he says, with a funky French accent, and she laughs out loud.

He opens a bottle of Sancerre white wine, and she reaches for the ring in the pocket of her pants and slips it on. As Henry raises his glass, he sees the ring, and his eyes open wide. And then she looks him straight in the eye.

"Listen to me, Snake, and listen, good. If you ever do that to me again, I swear I'll put a bullet right through your sorry butt. And you know I can do it."

"Ain't gonna happen, darlin'," he says. "I promise you that. I love you too much, Lily."

* * *

Henry's last concert in Montana is in Jefferson City. When the last set ends, the cheering and applause seem to go on forever. The audience knows that Snake and the River Rats are headed for the big time and have just released their first album. The cost of concert tickets will skyrocket in the next few months.

For over a year, true to his word, Henry does not wander. They buy December Ranch together, and Lily wins first place with Sugarbaby in the Carter County Equestrian Event and, for the second time, wins the Blue-Sky Sharpshooter Award. Henry goes on tour and calls her every night after his shows. They talk for hours, and he tells her he's writing another song for her. He sends her bouquets of calla lilies to remind her he adores her and promises to take a long break from the tour during the holiday season. She is happier than she's ever been. She is also pregnant.

* * *

Two days before his return, she gets a call from Annie, Tommy's girlfriend.

"Lily. I know it ain't my business, but I can't watch and let him make a fool outta you again."

Lily feels the bile in her throat. She immediately lays her hand on her tummy. She hasn't told him about the baby yet. Inhaling deeply several times, she asks, "What's going on, Annie?"

"Henry's messing around with Jess Watkins again. She's been following him on tour, and I saw him come out of her motel room this morning. I thought you should know. I'm so sorry."

Lily doesn't answer and ends the call.

She heads for the barn, walking quickly past the stalls. Her face is expressionless, but she is seething inside, and the tears are pouring from her eyes. She opens a large crate at the back of the outbuilding and pulls out a Ruger American rifle and a box of bullets.

* * *

A week later, Henry Withers is admitted to Rocky Mountain Hospital to remove a bullet from his right buttock. The bullet missed his spinal cord by one inch. Withers states he never saw it coming and claims he doesn't know who has cause to shoot him. Withers is also known as Snake, of Snake and the River Rats fame, and was scheduled to start his national tour in March.

The Portrait

I first met Kurt Wittelsbach at a Trustees fundraiser, on the grounds of the Alfred Allen-Woolsey Estate. He stood next to his wife, Marty, but his eyes followed the garden nymph, who wore a rhinestone mask, a nude leotard covered in white gardenias, and green and purple vinca that wound around her lithe body. As she flitted around the gardens, she bowed and pirouetted in the June twilight. With childlike wonder, Kurt laughed and began to clap. Marty quickly pushed his hands down, and his delight turned to shame.

Marty had invited me to the soiree as a thank-you for designing the invitations—miniature drawings of the estate from a larger watercolor I'd done for her the year before. I never knew what mood Marty would be in. One minute, she acted like my best friend, and the next time I saw her, she'd be distant and curt, making me wonder what I'd done wrong.

Everyone dressed as if it was a small wedding. I wore a long kelly-green skirt and ivory halter top with a faux emerald necklace I'd picked up at a thrift shop. I believe fashion does not have to put you in the poor house. I have to believe this because I'm a starving artist, living in an attic apartment and paying off college loans from ten years ago.

I'd heard about Kurt Wittelsbach before the party. Supposedly, he was of royal descent and an eccentric recluse. Some even said insanity ran in his family. He was rarely seen in public, so I was surprised to see him at the fundraiser. My first impression was a man of great stature. Tall and dignified, his posture was military straight, and he wore his black wavy hair combed back from his face. His dark eyes were large and curious, and a small goatee framed his wide mouth.

"Kurt. This is the woman from whom I bought the garden painting, Anna Morland."

"Anna, my husband, Kurt."

"How do you do, Ms. Morland," he said, bowing his head.

"Call me Anna, please," I said, looking up at him.

"Ahna," he pronounced it, which sounded exotic to me.

"Nice to meet you," I said. A waitress came by holding a platter of hors d'oeuvres. I hadn't eaten lunch, and my stomach grumbled like a bear in the woods. Holding a flute of champagne in my left hand, I picked up a napkin and toothpick with my right hand, then plucked a goat cheese and fig thingy. Dropping it on the ground, I bent to pick it up when Kurt gently put his hand on my arm to stop me. My face turned bright pink when Marty walked away. Kurt picked another hors d'oeuvre from the platter and held it out to me.

"Thank you," I said and popped it in my mouth before I dropped it again. After swallowing the damn thing, which wasn't worth the trouble, I turned around and looked at the gorgeous setting. "Feels like we're in a fairy tale here, doesn't it?"

"Yes!"

I was jarred by the exuberance of his response and started laughing. The colorful perennial flowers, stone walls, ornamental fountains, and tiny white lights twinkling throughout the gardens lent a whimsical feel to the estate. My awkward moment passed, and I was thankful to Kurt for ignoring my lack of grace.

"Maybe the butterflies talk when there's no one around."

Kurt put his hands together as if in prayer. "You possess a wonderful imagination, Ahna!" Eyes wide and hoping, he said, "Will you walk with me?"

"Okay."

Although it was a strange request from someone I just met, I was intrigued by the contrast between his reputation as a recluse and the childlike enthusiasm I was witnessing. I looked around for Marty, who was talking with a few guests by the greenhouse. I saw her glance at us and look away and wondered what she was thinking.

Kurt and I sauntered up and down the garden paths, admiring the flowers. There was little conversation, yet I felt a natural camaraderie as we bent and smelled our favorites. His eager boyishness was refreshing amid the other wealthy donors at the party. At one point, he lifted a gardenia between his fingers and inhaled deeply. "Ahh," he said with such drama that I laughed again, and he grinned.

"Those are my very favorites," I said, leaning closer and sniffing the white blossom. Strolling on, we took in the beauty of the calla lilies, deep blue delphiniums, and dark purple clematis winding through the latticework of an arbor.

"Do you have a garden, Ahna?"

"I wish. I don't even have a porch for potted plants."

"Where do you live?"

"In an attic apartment, I've lived in since I was a child with my mother."

"Does she still live with you?"

"No. She died three years ago. She had Alzheimer's."

"I'm very sorry."

"Thank you. She was very dear to me."

By the time we finished our walk, I felt like I'd known Kurt Wittelsbach for years. His easy, natural manner was comforting to me, and he'd made the party much more enjoyable than I'd hoped.

"Thank you, Ahna. That was lovely."

"Yes, it was. It was so nice to meet you."

He kissed my hand, and I felt like a princess.

* * *

For days, I couldn't stop thinking about Kurt Wittelsbach, his grandness, uninhibited pleasure in his surroundings, and our walk through the gardens. When the invitation came to visit their home on Gull Island for the weekend, I was not totally surprised. Somehow, I knew I would see him again.

I'd read about Castle Seehafen, the name of their estate when I saw a photo on the front cover of *Island Mansions.* It was a palace-like structure built of white limestone with turrets and chimneys and long windows. It reminded me of the Disney castle. Little did I know then it was purposely built in the likeness of King Ludwig II's castle in Bavaria.

I wondered how many others were invited for the weekend. I couldn't be the only one. I debated on calling Marty but I didn't know what to say. "Is this a special occasion? Can I bring anything?" I responded affirmatively and wanted to add an exclamation mark, but I figured that would be gauche. I went to my closet under the eaves and started trying on different outfits.

* * *

There was no one at the ferry landing when I arrived on Saturday afternoon. I looked at my watch and realized I was a few minutes early. At precisely two o'clock, a small boat pulled up to the pier. A man with a short, black beard and black beret that covered half his face asked if I was Anna Morland. He resembled Kurt, and I thought he might be a relation.

"Your bag," he said in a gruff voice, reaching his hand out.

"Thank you. Are you picking anyone else up?" I asked, wobbling into the dinghy.

"No."

"Beautiful day."

Nothing.

"Are you related to Kurt?" I asked, hoping to break through his wall.

"I'm his brother, Karl."

After that, he kept silent, and so did I. Seagulls soared and screeched above us, and the wind off the ocean was invigorating. Although I was nervous to be among the upper class, I was also thrilled to see Kurt again.

Twenty minutes later, we landed at the dock, where a small, older man waited on the sand to take my duffle bag and escort me to the house. He was wearing a suit and vest and had kind blue eyes. There was no one else around.

I followed him up a winding path made of crushed white seashells and lined on both sides with seven-foot-high dark red rhododendrons.

"Excuse me, sir. What is your name?"

"Ernst, Miss."

* * *

Although I'd seen pictures, I was anxious to see the house in person. But the walkway twisted and turned so often that the view was hidden until the last minute. Finally, we turned a corner, and there was the castle, and I felt as though I'd walked into another century.

"Oh my God," I whispered, coming to a dead stop. Ernst waited as I took it all in. "It's absolutely magnificent!" I took several photos as we approached the large double doors with the iron latches.

Kurt greeted me himself. "Hello, Ahna! Marty is running some last-minute errands, but she'll be here soon."

"Where is everyone?"

"They're not due for another hour. I wanted to speak with you alone first."

"Please," he said, leading me into an enormous hall, directing me toward the library.

"I am so happy to see you, Ahna. Have a seat. Can I get you some coffee or tea or a cold drink?"

"Water would be great." I looked around the tall ceilinged room lined with hundreds of books, their antique spines dusted and propped. It was then that I noticed the music playing in the background, a tender yet deeply passionate piece that filled me with an unusual longing.

"What is that you're listening to? The violins sound spiritual—sad yet so beautiful."

"A bit like life, wouldn't you say?"

"Yes." Already, Kurt and I were falling into a familiar banter.

"It's Richard Wagner's *Prelude to Lohengrin* about a knight who rescues a noblewoman in distress in a swan-driven boat."

"It's absolutely beautiful."

"I'm pleased that you like it. In fact, it's ironic that you mentioned it." He rang a bell from the mantle, and a large woman came into the room.

"Yes, sir?"

"Sigrid. Please get Miss Morland a glass of ice water, and I'll have the same."

I looked at the servant and said, "Hello, Sigrid. I'm Anna."

"Yes, Miss Anna."

"Now," Kurt said, rubbing his hands together. "I've already had the pleasure of owning several pieces of your artwork. And—"

"Several?"

"Why yes. The Alfred Woolsey piece and the one at Minton Gallery. I purchased the portrait of Lady Gaga as Queen Nefertiti. That's when I realized how wide your range of talent is."

"You bought that?"

He nodded. The portrait had sold for nine hundred dollars, and the buyer had remained anonymous.

"So," he continued, tenting his fingers, "I'd like you to do a portrait of me."

"*You?*"

"Yes. But you see I don't want a contemporary painting in American clothing. I want to be portrayed as King Ludwig II of Bavaria." He cleared his throat. "A distant relative."

"Oh wow!"

He then showed me a picture of the King in full regalia. I couldn't help but notice the similarities: dark, thick, wavy hair, goatee, arched eyebrows, and inquisitive eyes.

"They called him the Fairy Tale King, you know."

"No, I didn't know.

His eyes lit up. "In the middle of winter, in the middle of the night, he would have his horsemen drive him in the royal sleigh through the Alps. Can you think of anything more exhilarating?"

"It does sound fun."

"Have you ever heard of King Ludwig?"

"His name sounds familiar."

"You know more than you realize about him. You have already admired his favorite composer, Richard Wagner. And our Disney-like castle is a copy of Neuschwanstein, one of the many castles he built. And my favorite of all."

"I thought it looked like the Disney castle!"

Kurt gleefully clapped his hands, and I had a vision of Marty pushing his hands down at the soiree.

"So. You want your face in Ludwig's clothing and this same pose, right?" I asked, pointing at the picture.

Kurt covered his mouth and giggled, and I couldn't help but laugh with him. Kurt Wittelsbach as King Ludwig II. What a hoot.

"What is your commission for something like this?"

I hesitated. He certainly had the money. I looked again at the picture of King Ludwig and then at Kurt's face. I could do this and pay off my school loan.

"Six thousand dollars," I said, trying to act confident when, in fact, it would be the largest commission I'd ever received.

"Done." Kurt leaned back in his chair and sipped his ice water then placed it carefully on the side table.

"Unfortunately, King Ludwig was only forty years old when he died. As I grow older, I realize how short life is. Something he once said has remained in my mind."

"What's that?"

'I wish to remain an eternal enigma to myself and to others.' "I feel the same way," said Kurt, watching closely for my reaction.

As if reading my mind, he said, "You think I have an inflated ego? Tell me the truth, Ahna."

I hesitated. I didn't want to patronize him but it did sound a touch arrogant.

"I think it's more than just that. I think you have an unusually strong connection to Ludwig."

"Ah. The tactful Ahna. I suppose it is a bit narcissistic to think I'll live on in a painting of myself as Ludwig." Leaning over in his chair, he said, "But won't it be great fun?"

His joy was infectious, and I found him positively endearing.

"What is your actual relationship to Ludwig anyway?"

He paused, folding his lips in and looking at the ceiling. "I think he was my great-great-uncle something or other. Would you like to see the rest of the house before the others get here?"

"Yes, Your Highness."

"Oh Ahna, I love you already!"

Kurt held my hand as we walked out of the library, which seemed totally natural to me. Although he could have been my father, I felt like we were two children at play.

Turning left, I noticed one of my favorite paintings by Caspar David Friedrick—*Wanderer Above the Sea of Fog.*

"*Ruckinfigur,*" I said softly.

"Pardon?"

"*Ruckinfigur.* It means a figure seen from behind in a painting. The observer gazes out at what the person in the painting is looking at."

Kurt had his hands behind his back. "How intriguing."

"I will do your portrait in oil. It will give it a more compelling feel. What do you think?"

"Yes, Ahna. Quite so," he said, stroking his chin. "I'm so happy you understand my vision. Come, come. Let's tour the house before the other guests get here, and we have to behave."

Room by room, I saw the wealth and extravagance of the Wittelsbach family. In the sunroom, my painting of the Alfred-Allen Woolsey estate and gardens was prominently displayed over the gold velvet couch. I wondered where Lady Gaga as Nefertiti was; it didn't seem like the kind of art Marty would display.

Before Kurt and I came down the staircase, I was able to view twenty-three rooms, not including Sigrid and Ernst's apartment who were apparently married and lived on the third floor.

"Where does Karl live?"

"In the gatehouse. But he's a bit odd. Seriously, he's worse than me. He's practically deaf and runs around the estate shooting trees, especially when it's windy and the branches move. It spooks him. Marty can't bear him."

"If you don't mind me asking, why does he cover half his face with a beret?"

"He was a sniper for the German Army in Kunduz Province, fighting against the Taliban. His unit was bombed, and he was burned. He's lucky to have survived the explosion."

"How awful. I didn't realize Germany fought in Afghanistan. The poor man."

* * *

Kurt wanted to show me his room of castles, but we ran out of time. As we came down the stairs, Marty opened the door and came into the hall, carrying a large spray of fresh flowers.

"There you are," said Kurt. "I've been showing Ahna the house, and she has agreed to do my portrait!"

"Really. My husband's obsession with Ludwig is absurd. I hope you know what you're getting yourself into."

"Absolutely," I said cheerfully, just to piss her off.

Marty looked at the two of us as if we were co-conspirators in a murder. "I have to check on the staff." She looked at me in my white shirt and jeans and said, "Show Anna to her room so she can change in time for cocktails at five."

"Of course, dearest."

After Marty walked away, Kurt rolled his eyes and giggled. Marty seemed more like his mother than a wife to me.

My room was in the west wing of the castle and overlooked a lake. I hadn't expected to see a lake on a small island, but there it was, shimmering in the late afternoon light. In another hour, the sun would start making its descent and the magical colors of twilight would appear; my favorite time of day when I fell into a trance with no guidance.

The room was warm and elegant. Fit for a king, a dark mahogany four-poster bed with a hand-carved headboard and footboard stood against the wall to the right. The bed was covered in an ivory and gold-threaded satin spread, and I counted eight satin throw pillows in blue and gold. A Persian rug in shades of gold and blue covered the dark hardwood floor, and long pale gold drapes pooled on the floor. I smelled fresh-cut gardenias on the pedestal table; Kurt had remembered they were my favorite.

I opened the closet door, and an automatic light showed an empty walk-in closet. The other door led to a white marble bathroom with a clawfoot tub. I threw myself on the bed and looked up at the ceiling, imagining living like this all the time. How did someone like me end up in a palace like this?

I thought about the portrait I would soon be painting for Kurt. I reached for my tote bag, pulled out my computer, and Googled King Ludwig II. I became so fascinated in his story that I was almost late for cocktails. Looking at the clock, I closed my laptop and jumped off the bed.

I'd chosen several outfits to wear, depending on my mood: messy-rich, artsy, and elegant. My favorite hobby had always been dressing for special occasions on the cheap. When I was younger, my friend, Claudia, and I used to play dress-ups. We'd use scarves to wrap around our shoulders and wear her mother's old hats and high heels. We'd use her makeup and called ourselves Lydia and Tessa. We pretended we went to balls and imitated English accents, calling ourselves dahlink and laughing throughout our charade.

Living in an imaginary world at Claudia's house helped me escape the hardships of living in an attic apartment on the wrong side of town, where I shared a double bed with my mother. My father left when I was three, but I don't remember him at all. Mom was a waitress at Delvecio's six nights a week and cleaned houses three days a week. I did most of the cooking, which included tomato soup and melted cheese on toast, American Chop Suey, franks and beans, and macaroni and cheese from a box. Mom used to bring home leftovers from the restaurant whenever she could.

We might have moved to a bigger place, but when I showed an early talent as an artist, Mom started saving as much as possible to put me through art school. I babysat on weekends for the downstairs neighbor who also worked at Delvecio's. Her son, Thomas, was an intelligent four-year-old, and we used to color together. I taught him contour drawing and other various art techniques. Like me, his father had also left, and I felt a kinship with him. The last I heard, Thomas had won a school art competition. I like to think I had something to do with that.

After emptying my suitcase on the bed, I selected black satin palazzo pants and a pale lavender off-the-shoulder blouse. I twirled my dark hair into a bun at the nape of my neck, adding dangling rhinestone earrings and black stilettos—courtesy of the Salvation Army store. A touch of lavender eye shadow to accent my blue eyes, and *voila*! Before leaving the room, I remembered the gardenias and pinned a blossom behind my left ear. Though my stomach was fluttering, I was ready to meet the elite and pretend this was not my first rodeo.

* * *

"Good evening, Ernst," I said as he led me to the garden where cocktails were being served.

"Good evening, Miss Anna."

"This is quite the place, isn't it?"

A slight smile crossed his face, and his eyes twinkled. "Yes. It is."

"How long have you worked here?"

"I came to Boston from Munich thirty years ago when Mr. Wittelsbach was still a young man and hadn't built his castle yet. Not that he's old now, mind you. Here you go, Miss," he said, passing me a glass of champagne. "Feel free to mingle; they're actually a pretty good group," he said, winking.

Marty and Kurt stood in the middle of a crowd sipping drinks. Marty introduced me to her friend, Olivia, who stood close to her. A few couples had wandered down to the lake, some of them looking backwards at the castle in awe. Perhaps it was their first time seeing it, too. I walked up to my hosts and said hello.

"Ahna!" said Kurt. "You wore the gardenia! How is your room?"

"Gorgeous," I said. "This whole place is like a fantasy island."

Kurt looked as though he were going to clap but stopped himself, looking at Marty.

"That's because Kurt actually lives in a fantasy world," she said. "Why don't you two chat about your fantasies while I mingle with the other guests."

My mouth opened in awe at her rudeness.

157

"Come, let us talk," said Kurt. He set our glasses on the stone wall that enclosed the patio and guided me down to the lake.

"I Googled King Ludwig before I came downstairs," I said. "What an amazing story and such a mysterious end to his life. You have quite a resemblance to him."

His smile would have brightened an unlit ballroom. "Not only that, I relish many of the same things that Ludwig loved: isolation, fairy tales, castles, long walks, and dancing by myself."

I laughed and said, "As well as the composer, Richard Wagner?" I pronounced Wagner with a V to impress him. "I also saw a disturbing photo of King Ludwig and Dr. Gudden, who was with him when they both drowned. It's very eerie the way their bodies were bent over in four feet of water. And there was no water in Ludwig's lungs, meaning he was dead before submersion. What do you suppose really happened? Do you think Dr. Gudden had anything to do with it?"

"So many questions, Ahna. I see you have done quite a bit of research."

"It's captivating stuff and sounds a bit suspicious to me."

"To answer your question, I do believe King Ludwig was murdered by a member of the Bavarian ministry. He spent millions building his castles and sponsoring the career of Richard Wagner. His colleagues stated that Ludwig was insane based on intentional bias against him. The ministry imprisoned him at Castle Berg, and while trying to escape, he was shot twice in the back. Two bullet holes had gone through a gray coat, shirt, and vest—clothing that mysteriously disappeared."

It was then I heard several shots in the distance and assumed it was Karl shooting at trees. Whether it was from a breeze off the lake, or my own sense of foreboding, I felt a chill run through me.

"Are you cold, Ahna?"

"No, I'm fine," I lied.

"I think we should discuss the schedule for the portrait, yes?"

"Yes, of course. I'll need to take photographs of you and King Ludwig so I can make some sketches. Then you can choose the one you like best. You'll pose for me with breaks in between, but because it's oil, it will take longer to dry between applications. If all goes well, I'd guess the final product could be done in about forty hours. Then the paint needs to dry, so it'll be completely done in less than a month."

He stopped short, and a worried look crossed his face.

"What's wrong?" I asked.

"It has to be done sooner, Ahna."

"Why?"

He stamped his foot. "It just does!"

"Okay, okay. I'll do my best. What's your deadline?"

"A week from today."

I let out a groan. "Why the rush?"

His eyes filled with tears. "Please, Ahna."

"But I teach art classes to mentally challenged students on Mondays and Fridays, clean houses on Tuesdays and Thursdays, and work at the gallery on Wednesdays."

"Can't you find someone to cover for you just this once? Please? I'll give you another ten thousand dollars for your trouble." Kurt was staring at me with a tortured look I didn't understand.

"The oil will not be dry by then, Kurt."

"That's okay as long as it's completed."

"I suppose I could add linseed oil and put it directly in the sun. But that's the best I can do."

"Excellent!"

"But the schedule is tight." I felt stressed as I tried to work out a schedule in my mind to finish the most important painting I'd ever done in a week's time. My students looked forward to the classes and would be disappointed, but it was only for two days, and then I would be back.

"Alright. I'll need to leave tomorrow morning and return in the afternoon with my art supplies. I'll take the photos and do the sketches here tomorrow night."

This time, he did clap. "You are my angel, Ahna."

"It's going to take an angel to do this in a week, Your Majesty."

* * *

That night at dinner, Kurt tried to bring up the portrait, but Marty quickly shut him down.

"Kurt. Not now," she said abruptly, and I saw the anger in his face. Her friend, Olivia, put her hand on Marty's arm. For the rest of the night, Kurt did not speak to anyone. He left the table before dessert, and I heard the mumbling among the guests.

"How she puts up with him, I'll never know."

"He acts like a child."

"I thought he was going to throw his drink at her."

"The guy's nuts, everyone knows that."

I figured Kurt was in the library, and when the others left to wander, I knocked on his door.

When he opened it, he smiled. "Ahna." *Lohengrin's Prelude* was playing softly in the background.

"Are you okay?"

"Yes, of course. I'm just having another one of my headaches."

I stepped into the room and saw that several books had been thrown against the fireplace, their pages scattered across the hearth. A glass vase also lay broken. I said nothing and sat down. Sigrid came into the room and offered coffee, completely ignoring the mess Kurt had made.

"No, thank you," said Kurt, waving her away.

"Thank you for asking, Sigrid."

"Why are you so friendly to the servants, Ahna?"

His question took me off guard.

"Because my mother worked her entire life in service as a waitress and cleaning houses. She worked very hard to put me through art school, and I will never forget what she did for me. People were often rude and treated her shamefully."

"You have a good heart, Ahna. You probably know Ludwig and his cousin, SiSi, were great friends. She was really his only true friend and was loyal to the very end. She even tried to help him escape. I hope you consider me *your* friend, Ahna."

It made me sad that he had to ask.

"Of course I do."

I returned to my room and read more about Ludwig until my eyes became heavy. I looked at my watch. It was four o'clock in the morning. I had become fascinated by this complicated King whose ministry had covered up the real facts of his death. Among Ludwig's other nicknames were Mad King Ludwig, The Swan King, and the Dream King. I pondered whether he was certifiably insane as the ministry had accused him—or if he was just eccentric. Unfortunately, we'll never really know.

Kurt was not at the breakfast buffet the next morning. I wasn't surprised. From what I observed, Kurt possessed a sensitive nature, and Marty was a cold fish.

"Anna—may I speak with you privately?" Marty asked as I was leaving the breakfast room.

"Sure," I said and followed her out to the garden. It was a windy day, and Karl was shooting trees in the backwoods.

"Oh, for God's sake," Marty mumbled.

We sat in Adirondack chairs facing the lake. "By now, you must realize that my husband is a strange man," she said, staring straight ahead. "He is also a handsome, older, rich man and very charming when he wants to be."

I did not know where this was going and did not respond.

Marty placed her hand on my arm, and her voice softened. "I understand your reluctance to talk against your sponsor. Obviously, you are going to make a great deal of money on this commission. But be careful, Anna. You are young and impressionable, and someone like Kurt can be very persuasive. He's also delusional."

Still, I said nothing. I knew Kurt was different, yet I found him enchanting at the same time. He was a boy in a man's body. So what? What harm was he to anyone? And Marty was clearly benefitting from his fortune.

"My advice to you is to finish the portrait and go away from here, or he will break your heart."

Without thinking, I said, "Did he break your heart, Marty?"

She stood up and looked down at me. I was surprised at the sorrow in her eyes.

"Poor Anna. You are so naïve and already lost in his lunacy." And then she left without another word.

* * *

I sat there, staring out at the lake. Was I really that young and impressionable? What did she mean when she said he would break my heart? Did she think I was in love with him?

Kurt found me sitting there, and when he touched my shoulder, I jumped. "What are you thinking, Ahna?"

"I'm thinking I need to leave now in order to return later. Please make arrangements to take me back to the mainland as soon as possible. I think Kurt's out shooting, it's breezy, but could you have him meet me back at the ferry at four when I'll have my easel and supplies with me. And please find me the sunniest and driest room in the castle."

"I will take care of it immediately."

Whether or not Marty would still be there, I didn't ask. Nor did I care.

* * *

As it turned out, I stayed at the Castle for seven days until the thirteenth of June. Marty had left with Olivia. Some would say I was asking for trouble, a young woman alone except for a few servants, with a man who Marty had called a lunatic. But my relationship with Kurt was never sexual, not even close. It was true I had become caught up in his world, his castle, and his dream of channeling the spirit of King Ludwig on canvas. But I had the ability to make his dream come true, and I would keep my word.

I returned on Sunday night and finished the sketches in the library. Kurt pointed to the east windows where the best lighting would be. At approximately nine o'clock the next morning, I heard the door open, and in walked Kurt in full costume.

I stared open-mouthed at his dashing appearance. A bright red sash ran from his left shoulder down to his waist, and various medals were pinned to his royal blue jacket, which was belted at the waist. He wore white breeches with tall black boots and a white fur cape draped from his shoulders to the floor. It looked as if he had teased his hair and sprayed it in the very likeness of the King.

"King Ludwig!" I cried out. "How nice to see you!"

"Oh, Ahna, I have counted the hours!"

We both laughed. I handed him the charcoal sketches, then sipped the coffee he'd brought for me.

"These are magnificent, Ahna!"

He handed me the one he wanted and said, "I couldn't have asked for a better likeness!"

"But you want the portrait done from the waist up, right?"

"Yes, yes. I just wanted you to see me in full dress so I could have the same royal feeling as Ludwig did when he posed."

I nodded and began to paint.

Needing to be as confident as possible in order to speed up the process, my eyes drifted from Kurt's face to Ludwig's and back again. Slowly, Kurt, as the King, came to life on canvas. I found myself questioning whether I was painting Kurt as King Ludwig or King Ludwig as Kurt. I thought about the original artist, Ferdinand von Piloty, who had done the original King Ludwig's portrait back in 1865. Had he thought King Ludwig mad then? Or did he adore him as many in his kingdom once had—maybe both?

I had not planned on becoming so fascinated with Ludwig, but the research had triggered my imagination, his mistrust of people in general, and his infatuation with building castles all over Bavaria. In many ways, he truly was a fairy tale king. He dressed in the swan knight costume in Wagner's opera *Lohengrin* and danced and sang by himself in his rooms. He was nocturnal, sleeping until six o'clock in the evening, then staying up all night. Strange as it was, he supposedly once dined with his horse.

I became lost in my work while Kurt stared to the left, like Ludwig had once done before him.

Hours later, after several breaks, I said, "That's enough for today." I had worked so intently that my arm ached, and I rubbed it after I put my brush down.

"Can I see it?"

"No, you cannot."

The pout on his face reminded me of four-year-old Thomas when I told him it was bedtime.

"We'll need another sitting tomorrow and maybe the next day."

"Wonderful! I'll go change, and then we can have something to eat."

Kurt nearly skipped from the room and I turned to look again at the portrait. Who was who?

After a light supper, Kurt wanted to show me his room of castles. Built by a Boston architect and spread out on an oval table that nearly filled the room were miniature castles based on those Ludwig II had built. His castle in the Bavarian Alps, Schloss Neuschwanstein, Schloss Linderhof, where he lived during the last eight years of his life, and Schloss Herrenchiemsee, inspired by King Louis XIV of France. Even the lakes and mountains, lawns, and landscaping were created with real water, turf, and dirt, as well as a working fountain that spouted real spray when he pressed a button.

"These castles are all open to the public now," said Kurt proudly. "I have seen all of them, and they are much more beautiful in person."

"I can't believe the detail." I kept walking around the table, admiring every feature and characteristic of each castle.

"But what about Seehafen? Will you add that to your collection?"

"Sadly, no. There's not enough—"

"Not enough what?"

He had to think for a moment. "Room! There's not enough room."

I had the sense he was keeping something from me, but I had no idea what. I started to yawn and apologized. "I have to get some sleep, Kurt."

"Yes, I feel another headache coming on. Good night, Ahna."

As I climbed the curved staircase, I wondered if he'd sneak a look at the portrait, which I'd turned around and placed in the corner. As I reached the second landing, I felt unsettled, blaming it on being over-tired as I opened my bedroom door.

I continued to paint for the next few days as Kurt sat perfectly still. I knew it was killing him not to see it, but until I brushed the last stroke, he would have to wait.

* * *

Late Wednesday night, I heard something banging down the hall. Slipping on a short robe, I left my room and went out to the corridor. It was coming from Kurt's room. I knocked on his door, but there was no answer. I turned the doorknob and found Kurt lying on the floor, slamming his head in a fitful seizure. I rushed over and knelt beside him as he moaned and bit his tongue.

"It's okay, Kurt. It's okay," I said, not knowing what to do. Gradually, he came out of the convulsion but had soiled his pajamas. He lay there helpless, and I did not want him to know I had witnessed his lack of dignity. As I left the room, I noticed the painting of Lady Gaga as Nefertiti on his wall. And then I went looking for Ernst, who was already coming downstairs from his room. I started to say something, and he shook his head no.

"Go back to bed, Miss Anna. I'll take care of him." I knew then it was not the first time Kurt had had a seizure and that Ernst was well aware of it. I assumed it was epilepsy.

* * *

On Thursday of the same week, I finished the portrait of Kurt as King Ludwig. I laid my paintbrush on the tray of my easel and sat back with my hands on my lap.

"Is it ready, Ahna? Is it?"

"Yes. It is." I smiled, pleased with the result. Kurt rushed over and covered his mouth. He laughed with glee and hugged me.

"You've done it by God. There I am, as I was meant to be!"

And then he danced around the room, twirling and trying to do splits in the air. I laughed at his dancing, but more importantly, I laughed at the happiness I had brought him.

And then he suddenly stopped dancing—and burst out crying.

"Kurt! What's wrong?"

"Ahna. I must share a terrible secret with you so that you know why this portrait means so much to me."

"What is it, Kurt?"

"Please. Sit here with me on the window seat."

For a long time, we watched day's departure and night's arrival. Then he held my hand.

"I'm dying, Ahna."

My heart started pounding, and I thought it would burst from my chest. "Oh my God. How can that be? What's wrong?"

"I have a large brain tumor and only a few weeks at best. My headaches and seizures are worsening."

I bowed my head, and the tears spilled down my cheeks. "I'm so sorry. I'm so very, very sorry."

"That is why your portrait means so much. I have long believed I am related to King Ludwig. He reminded me so much of myself: his playful, strange behavior, his love of Wagner's music."

"He was a fascinating man for sure," I said, the tears still flowing.

"Don't cry, Ahna. I'm at peace with it. But I do have a grave request that you do not have to agree to, if you'd rather not."

"Anything."

"I would like to drown in the lake, in four feet of water, the same as Ludwig did, on the very same day."

"*What?*"

"I've been saving the medication I'm supposed to take for pain. But I would like you to be at my side when I take the final dose."

"You want me to aid in your suicide?"

"I want you to be with me when I die. Please think about it. I can no longer stand the pain."

"I don't think I can do that, Kurt."

"I understand."

* * *

A jumble of nerves, after dinner, I went upstairs to lay down. Why had Kurt chosen me to be with him when he died? Why not Ernst? Or Sigrid or Karl? Why had our paths crossed only to end in this horrible way?

It wasn't wrong for him to want to die on his own terms, especially because he was suffering. Then I thought of my mother and how I had watched her die slowly from Alzheimer's, unable to recognize me at the end. Feeding tubes, diapers, nothing but a penciled sketch of what she used to be. Every day, I watched her die a little more, and there was nothing I could do for her. If she had been able to talk and understand her illness, would she have asked me to help her die? I have asked myself that so many times since she passed away. I think I know what she would have wanted.

* * *

At precisely six fifty-four in the evening, on June thirteenth, the same date and time King Ludwig II had drowned in Lake Starnberg over one-hundred-thirty years ago, I walked down the hall and looked out the window. Kurt was standing in the lake dressed as King Ludwig. My heart tightened at his solitary figure, and I knew then I couldn't let him die alone. He started to lift a bottle of pills when I knocked on the window fiercely, shaking my head no. Then I turned and ran down the stairs as fast as I could.

'Kurt! Wait!"

I ran to his side and held his arm.

"Dear Ahna," he slurred, "You came. I wish we had met years ago...had more... together." And then he emptied the pills into his mouth. I prayed I would not faint as my legs wobbled, and I stared straight ahead. The tears came fast as I felt his body slump into the water.

* * *

Sigrid and Ernst came running out of the house and held me while I sobbed.

"Anna, we need to talk to you before you leave. You may want to sign some papers."

"What are you talking about?"

"Please come into the house."

We walked into the large kitchen and sat at the long wood table while Sigrid made coffee. Karl was standing across the room, leaning against the counter.

"Anna," Sigrid began. "You know Kurt was never related to King Ludwig II, right?"

"Yes, in my heart I knew. But there was such a remarkable resemblance it was hard to believe he wasn't."

Ernst looked at me knowingly. "His real name is Kurt Christoph Bauer Wasselberg. He was born in Füssen, Bavaria, and at fifteen, started showing signs of a psychiatric disorder known as grandiose delusions soon after his mother's death, which prompted a change in his personality. He was always a high-strung child, and he was very close to his mother. Inconsolable after she died, he visited Neuschwanstein and saw his resemblance to the young King Ludwig II."

"Who was his mother?" I asked.

"Freya Carina nee Bauer Wasselberg. She was the heiress to the Munich Beer Company fortune and died of colon cancer."

"What about his father?"

Ernst looked at Sigrid, who nodded.

"He died years before his mother when he had a heart attack in bed with his mistress."

"And you've been with them ever since?"

"Yes. Sigrid and I were appointed executor of the estate, and we adopted both boys legally."

"When did you change their names?"

"We never did. We came to America and simply allowed the boys to use the family name of King Ludwig II-Wittelsbach. The psychiatrist told us that sometimes, when you give in to a patient's delusions, it can help their self-esteem.

"What about you, Karl?"

He laughed. "I was the spare. It was Kurt who inherited all the money."

I had assumed Karl's oddness was due to injuries in Afghanistan. But did he possibly have a mental disorder, too?

"And Marty knew all the time?"

"We made a deal," said Sigrid, placing the coffee cups on the table. "Marty kept her maiden name and signed a prenuptial, which gave her a substantial amount of money for her art collection, charities, and personal use. She also had her own reason for the cover-up. People would assume Kurt was really a distant relative of King Ludwig II, which would keep him happy; Marty's lover, Olivia, would remain her private business."

"Then why did she publicly humiliate him? How was that keeping her end of the deal?"

"It wore her down," said Ingrid.

I kept silent.

"We did not count on Kurt becoming so enamored of you. However, you made him a very happy man in the last days of his life. And you will be compensated."

"I've already been compensated."

"Not completely. I'll get the papers, Ernst," she said and left the room.

I looked out the window at the lake. Had his body sunk yet? Would it float? And did it really matter now if I'd unwittingly played a role in his delusion? Hadn't I known it was true without it ever being confirmed?

Sigrid came back into the kitchen and laid a folder in front of Ernst, The Last Will and Testament of Kurt Christoph Bauer Wasselberg.

"Rather than go through all the technicalities," said Ernst, "it basically bequeaths the gatehouse where Karl now lives to you. Karl prefers to go back to Munich, and he has been left a substantial amount of money. Ernst and I will stay here at Castle Seehafen. It also states that, should you agree, you will create The Kurt Wittelsberg Art Foundation for The Mentally Challenged here at the Castle, where you will teach art classes. Kurt was well aware of your dedication to the mentally challenged. Many of the rooms will be open to the public, and the proceeds will go towards the Foundation."

They all looked at me. My mouth was open, shocked by the revelation that Kurt had left not just a great responsibility in my hands, but was also giving me a real home.

With a weighty heart, I agreed to the terms and signed the papers.

"By the way, what does Seehafen actually mean?" I asked, rising from the chair.

"Lake haven," Sigrid said softly.

* * *

Rumors still continue as to Kurt Wittelsbach's demise. Some say I was his mistress and gave him an overdose of barbiturates in order to inherit his estate. I don't care what anyone thinks anymore.

I moved into the gatehouse, a charming cottage in the woods with wood beams and small-paned windows, a quaint kitchen with shutters that opened to a lake view, and beautiful hardwood floors. A framed picture of my mother sits on the mantle of the stone fireplace in the sitting room. Gardenias are delivered to the cottage once a month, reminding me of a walk through a garden on a beautiful June day and how a man who believed he was a king—changed my life forever.

The Burren

Florence was on her third glass of Guinness, and her face was flushed. Ronald watched her across the table as the spider-like vessels across her nose became inflamed. Soon, her entire face and neck would be blotched.

He tried to imagine thirty more years with her. Thirty more years of putting his obese, boozing wife to bed, waking her from alcohol-induced naps. He'd become her caretaker, nothing more than an enabler of her addiction. After weeks of pleading and coaxing her to get away from their estate in West Kent, she'd finally agreed to come to Ireland, but only for two days. Two days to make a decision that would change his life forever.

The waiter served their food and Ronald kept studying Florence. When she bent down to eat, he could see the pink of her scalp through the tight, blonde, and gray curls. She was fifty-two years old, and to him, she looked seventy. Her breasts sagged and the emerald earrings and pendant, family jewels she wore dutifully, did nothing to enhance her appearance. She reminded him of the Queen, gray and sexless.

For the past ten years, Ronald had watched as she deteriorated, watching her disinterest in everything but food, drink, and a Tabby cat. She had eliminated any form of outside entertainment from her mundane life. Would she care to see a play in the West End over the weekend? How about The Hampton Court Flower Show? Lunch at Harrods?

"No! No! No!" she answered every time he suggested something that might interest her.

Although he could barely contain his contempt for her sometimes, he was still baffled as to why she seemed to have just given up on life. She'd had everything—family money, education, parents who had doted on her as their only child, and Ronald, who had once loved her. Yet she had still grown languid and vinegary.

"I must say The Burren is a poor representation of a country known for its pastoral beauty," Florence was saying. "Why can't we go to the Cliffs of Moher? Or Blarney Castle? Why do you have to pick the ugliest part of the country? There's nothing there but rocks. I don't understand you sometimes, Ronald."

Had she ever? He wondered.

"Darling," he said, "Do try and appreciate the archaeological history. The Burren was formed millions of years ago, and there are over a hundred miles of Bronze Age tombs, an abbey from the 12th century called Corcomroe, and the Poulnabrone Dolmen, a tomb that dates back to 2900 BC. Florence," he said, leaning over the table, "You can walk for miles and never see a soul."

"Well, I'm not walking anywhere."

Ronald took a deep breath. "I realize it seems like just a vast expanse of rock, but it's quite remarkable, actually."

She dismissed him with a wave of her hand.

"Only to you, Ronald. This is 1999—not the Bronze Age. Try and think of someone else for a change," she continued. "You and your history, nobody *cares*."

He watched the remnants of her shepherd's pie seep out of the right corner of her mouth. He pointed to his mouth, and she used her napkin.

"It's all rather boring, Ronald. You should live in the present. Now, do something useful and order me another Guinness."

Today was the first time in a long time that Ronald and Florence had had any type of conversation. Usually, Ronald read the paper, and Florence made a project out of eating and drinking. She was the only woman he'd ever known who could drink herself to sleep at the table.

"You used to like history. What changed, Florence?"

"I lost interest, is all," she said, flinging her hand and nearly knocking over her glass.

"Isn't there *anything* that interests you? What about reading? I never see you with a book anymore."

"What is this, Ronald? Why all the questions?"

"I'm just trying to make conversation with you, Florence. We never talk like this. We just eat our meals together, watch the telly, and go our separate ways."

"Are you bored, dear? Bored with all my money?"

He let out a sigh. "You really don't understand, do you?"

"What's there to understand?"

"We're still young, Florence. We're only in our fifties, for God's sake, and we live like two people in a home for the aged. We never take walks together, discuss books or the news, or anything for that matter."

"You're spoiled, Ronald. You want everything like the little boy you still are. It could be worse. You could be back at Claridge's, carrying valises and collecting tips."

"I know that. You've been awfully generous to me, and I appreciate it."

That much was true. Orphaned at thirteen, Ronald had grown up in Manchester, a mining town north of London, where he ran errands and did odd jobs to survive. He'd slept in coal sheds and rundown stables of neighbors who took pity on him after his mother died of pneumonia and his father of black lung disease.

Florence spooned more pie into her mouth. Ronald gazed out the window. It was early May, and outside was a green meadow with scattered purple and white wildflowers. A group of alder trees provided shade, and several horses grazed by the trees. Every so often, their tails twitched to keep the flies away.

He turned back to Florence and said, "Traveling makes *me* happy. Reading history books, visiting museums, dining out, and meeting new people makes me happy. Having someone to share those things with would be even nicer, Florence."

"Oh, grow up, Ronald. You're a bloody dreamer. You should be thankful for the life you have. People who've been married as long as we have don't go gallivanting around the globe, flaunting their wealth."

"It's not a matter of flaunting your wealth. It's a matter of enjoying what you have," he said, taking a sip of his scotch.

"I enjoy what I have just the way it is."

"Do you really, Florence? *What* do you enjoy?"

"Oh bloody hell. I enjoy a tall gin and tonic, a nice rack of lamb and an apple treacle, satisfied?" she asked raising eyebrows that hadn't been plucked in decades. She emptied her glass of Guinness and raised her arm, snapping her fingers at the waiter and pointing to her glass.

The waiter served Florence another drink and moved to the next table, where a younger couple was smiling and holding hands. Ronald watched them, remembering when he and Florence had first been in love. He'd moved to London when he was seventeen and worked as a valet at Claridge's. With his good looks and engaging personality, he soon attracted members of the upper class. He learned how to speak proper English and read Chaucer and Joyce, Yeats, and Carroll. He pursued his love of history, reading books recommended by hotel guests on Napoleon, Julius Caesar, and Alexander the Great.

He became friendly with an American tycoon named Richard LaPierre, who told him, "Opportunities are scarce, and you will do well to take advantage of every one of them."

And then Ronald Niven had seen his opportunity—in an heiress named Florence Denison. He had loved her then, although her friends thought their relationship was a cliché: handsome nobody snags rich wife. When both her parents had died in a car crash, she'd leaned on Ronald and found solace in their relationship. He had hoped to have a family with her. Sons and daughters who would have the things he never had, who would never worry about where their next meal was coming from, children who would be well-educated and to whom he could read stories of Napoleon's conquests and Caesar's doom. But Florence was as barren as The Burren. He'd wanted to adopt children, but she had refused adamantly.

"I'll not be saddled with someone else's castoff. Who knows whose genes they'll have."

It was only a few years before they settled into a dull country life. Day after day, week after week, month after month, Ronald walked for miles to keep busy. He sat on hillsides, beside streams, and under trees, alone, reading and wondering how long he could sustain this way of life.

He looked back at Florence, who was stuffing soda bread in her mouth.

If only she had listened to him more, taken part in a world outside of their estate and a bottle of Beefeater's. They had no friends and only distant relatives most of whom had moved to Scotland and the States. Whenever he tried to interact with other people, she had always discouraged it.

"I don't like the Blackburns," she'd said when he told her he'd talked to them on one of his walks. "I never did—they're unrefined."

"Their daughter, Emma, is quite nice," Ronald said. "She's full of life and quite worldly for someone in her early twenties. She loves to read, and I've leant her a few of my books."

Looking at him in horror, she'd said, "Not from the Denison Library, I hope!"

"Never," he'd said, placing his hand over his heart.

* * *

"What happened to you, Florence?" he asked softly. "Why did you just stop caring about life? About me?"

"Oh, for God's sake, Ronald, stop this psychological drivel and eat your pork!"

Several customers looked over at the table, but Ronald no longer cared.

"I just want to know," he insisted. "Was it because we never had children?"

Florence sprayed Ronald with her spit as she hissed at him, "Stop it this minute. What's gotten into you? I didn't come here to be cross-examined."

"I'm just talking about a *life*, Florence. All the money in the world can't replace loneliness and the need for companionship."

"If that's true, Ronald, why haven't you asked me for a divorce?"

"I'd hoped things would change."

"Rubbish. Money makes all the difference in the world to you. Don't fool yourself, Ronald, you want it all and you can't have it. Divorce would leave you penniless."

* * *

Ronald looked down at his plate. So, there it was—a divorce that would leave him with nothing—or die slowly. Why had he even bothered to find common ground with her? Was it a last, desperate attempt to ease his guilt so that he could tell himself one day that he'd tried right up until the end?

Florence sat up straight and took a deep breath. And then a hollow, guttural echo, most unladylike, erupted.

"Pardon me," she said, looking surprised at the voracity of her expulsion. She gazed at Ronald, hoping he had calmed down, but he was staring off into space. A half-hour later, Florence and Ronald left the pub, Florence staggering and leaning heavily on Ronald's arm.

"There you go," he said, pushing her head down under the roof of the car. "Mind your head. That's my girl. Now, have yourself a little nap."

* * *

Ciarán Devlin was a Tinker, a member of the Travelling People who'd been roaming Ireland since the Middle Ages. He spoke Shelta, a language indistinguishable from those outside the group. He was almost seven feet tall, and his black hair hung in matted clumps to his shoulders. When he was agitated, his black eyes darted back and forth as if frightened by his own emotions. But when he held a small bird in the palm of his hand or played tag with the children, his eyes reflected an innocent joy.

The caravan was parked on the edge of The Burren, but Ciarán liked to wander from the camp and explore the landscape. He wore a threadbare tailcoat whose sleeves only reached his elbows and a pair of pants that were too short. An odd, gangling figure, he weaved and swayed as he walked and mumbled incoherently.

* * *

After Ronald had strapped Florence in and closed the door, he leaned against the car and smoked a cigarette. In a few minutes, his once lovely, aristocratic wife would be snoring and drooling onto her shoulder like the old boiler she'd become. It seemed now that their whole life together had all passed by too quickly, and he was surprised at the tinge of sadness he felt.

She'd been nice-looking once, petite with soft grey eyes and a sweet smile. She was a willing partner in bed and had surprised Ronald with her enthusiasm. They had traveled to Greece, Spain, and Switzerland. He remembered when she held on to him as they rode the cable car up the Matterhorn glacier. He'd felt strong and needed by her.

He lit another cigarette and thought of the day he'd found her in the guest room with Meadow, her Tabby cat. She was stroking the cat gently from the top of its head to the end of its tail while it purred in her lap. He hadn't heard, in a long time, the soft and loving tone she was using.

"You're Mummy's little baby, aren't you Meadow? Mummy's baby girl, who loves her more than anyone else in the whole wide world."

Then she'd picked the cat up and put it over her shoulder as if she were going to burp it. Florence hadn't noticed him standing by the doorway and he'd backed away.

There was no use thinking of what might have been now. It was too late. He flicked his cigarette and got back in the car as a feeling of failure and dread overcame him.

* * *

Ronald drummed his long, slender fingers on the steering wheel, clinking his wedding ring nervously. He looked over at Florence, whose face was mashed against the window.

He drove for thirty minutes, passing the Poulnabrone Dolmen, a megalithic tomb where, in 1986, the remains of 33 people had been unearthed, some of them dating back to 3,800 B.C. Florence twisted and farted in her sleep, and he put the window down.

* * *

Ciarán had climbed the hill and looked out over the vast terrain. The sun was lowering in the sky. Soon, the campfires would start, and so would the drinking and the dancing. But he did not want to go back. He sat down, his long legs stretched in front of him. Then, he leaned against a rock and fell asleep.

* * *

Ronald slowed the car, stopping where a wide, dirt path led to the top of a small, craggy mount of boulders and sharp rocks. On both sides of the path, as far as the eye could see, layered limestone spanned the landscape with an occasional patch of wildflowers. The history and vastness of his surroundings intrigued him even though it was desolate. He thought of his life—isolated and joyless, until he'd met Judith.

He'd first seen her at the British Museum two years earlier. She was standing in front of a Parthenon statue of a horse's head, and he was struck by her stillness and composure as she stared at the sculpture. He walked up and stood beside her.

"Do you think the Greeks should get their sculptures back?"

She'd turned and looked at him with blue steel eyes and said, "Not on your life." She'd smiled, and they had moved along the statues together and then to the next room and the room after that. They talked about each artifact, and he was amazed at her knowledge of history. She was American, and everything about her was elegant, her clothes, her makeup, her voice, even her hands. She was married, and she, too, was unhappy.

* * *

Ronald chose the most remote part of the region and parked the car, checking for any signs of life. But The Burren was as silent as the tombs beneath it.

Ronald was not a cruel person by nature; therefore, it was not his intention that Florence should suffer in any way. Swiftly and nimbly, he pulled on a pair of leather gloves and then grabbed the .22 caliber High Standard pistol from under his seat. He turned toward Florence and angled the gun in her left ear, firing off two quick shots. Although her body jolted from the impact, she had been unconscious and never felt a thing. He leaned back, twisting to the right, located the two shell cases in the back seat, and put them in his pocket. Then he got out of the car.

He removed his jacket and laid it on the seat. Rolling up his shirtsleeves, he went to the trunk, where inside was a green canvas tarp, rope, and a crowbar. His heart was pounding, and his hands shook as he pulled them out. He looked up at the dark clouds hovering over him, witnessing what he was doing, daring him to get away with it.

He left Florence in the car and headed up a dirt path with the crowbar. Ten minutes later, he found what he was looking for and began prying away a large boulder with enough space to place a body. His shirt was soaked with sweat, and he pulled a handkerchief from his pocket to wipe his face. Then he sat down to rest, breathing hard. He returned to the car, dragged Florence to the tarp, and wrapped her tightly, securing her body with a rope at both ends. But not before he'd removed her precious jewels.

Grunting and sweating, he dragged the tarp up over the rocks and stuffed her body inside the opening he'd created. Then he pushed the boulder back in place. He sat down again on a rock to rest, staring at Florence's burial place.

"Sorry, old girl," he said. "I'd hoped it wouldn't come to this."

He lit a cigarette and gazed out over The Burren. He thought of Florence lying still under the boulders of The Burren for eternity. He took a deep breath and crushed out his cigarette then put it in the pocket of his jacket.

"Goodbye, Florence. Sorry I couldn't bury Meadow with you."

He got back into the car and drove to the ferry at Rosslare, tossing the gun and shell cases into the Irish Sea en route to Fishguard. Though he'd paid cash for the ferry, their meals, and for one night of lodging in Rosslare, leaving no paper trail, Ronald had still held out hope that they could come to an amicable settlement. When Florence had told him he'd be penniless if they divorced, she'd left him with little choice.

The next day, he was back at his country estate in West Kent. The entire staff had been given a three-day pass to celebrate the Queen's birthday. No one had any idea that Ronald and Florence had ever left the country.

* * *

Detective Chief Inspector John Bodmin of the West Kent Police watched the couple from across the room. He was sitting in the Terrace Room at Harrods and recognized the man who had reported his wife missing only two days before. He did not recognize the woman, but she was very beautiful, a ringer for Sharon Stone.

Bodmin was forty-seven years old, ran three miles a day, and maintained a strict diet. He was not easily fooled and had a reputation for never letting go of a case, no matter how cold it was. Relentlessness was his forte and had earned him the nickname "Bullhead."

Bodmin had checked Niven's financial records and credit card information. There were no charges for car rentals, hotels, food, liquor, or other incidentals over the past week. They had searched his estate in Penshurst and the surrounding townships, including dragging the River Medway, but Florence Niven's body had still not been found. Bodmin interviewed neighbors who described Mr. Niven as a perfect gentleman and dependable husband, although they did not see much of Mrs. Niven. The only thing the police found of interest was a brochure of The Burren wedged in the passenger side pocket of their Jaguar.

Niven's chilly response to Bodmin's question of how much he would inherit from Florence's estate was snobbery, but his theatrical surprise when Bodmin told him she was worth over three million pounds was dubious. Even more so was Niven's story of Florence's disappearance. He'd gone for a long walk and when he came home, she was gone? A woman who rarely leaves her home does not suddenly vanish without a trace.

"She was a depressed alcoholic, I'm afraid," he told Bodmin.

"*Was* Mr. Niven?"

Niven had cleared his throat. "I mean, there's no telling where she might have gone."

Bollocks, thought Bodmin, and decided to follow his prime suspect.

* * *

Dabbing the corners of his mouth with his napkin, he paid the check and approached Niven's table. Nothing like the element of surprise, he thought.

"Good afternoon, Mr. Niven. I trust you're faring well."

Niven's shocked look was enough to bring a glint to Bodmin's eyes. Bodmin observed the champagne bottle resting in an ice bucket.

"Why, Detective Bodmin, what a pleasant surprise!"

Bodmin gazed down at the woman.

"Judith, this is Detective Chief Inspector John Bodmin from the West Kent police. Mr. Bodmin, Judith Linnane, a friend from the States."

Bodmin bowed slightly, taking in the diamond bracelet, manicured nails, and Chanel purse.

"How do you do, Ms. Linnane."

"Fine, thank you, Mr. Bodmin."

"I trust you are enjoying your stay in London?"

"Very much so."

"What part of the States are you from, Ms. Linnane?"

Judith smiled. "Texas."

"I see. Might I inquire where in Texas?"

"Oh, I've lived all over the state, Mr. Bodmin, Houston, Austin, Dallas."

"And now, Ms. Linnane? Where do you live now?"

Ronald shifted in his seat.

"Actually, I'm in transit right now, Mr. Bodmin."

Bodmin smiled. "Well. I won't keep you. I just wanted to say hello. It was nice to meet you, Ms. Linnane. Good Day, Mr. Niven."

"Good Day, Bodmin," said Ronald, reaching for his glass.

Bodmin drove back to West Kent, trying to figure out how Niven had pulled it off.

* * *

They hadn't eaten when Judith asked for another bottle of champagne, already tipsy from the first. She'd knocked over a small vase of flowers, which the waiter had promptly replaced. When she'd started to slur her words, Ronald became queasy. Then he watched as her porcelain skin slowly began to flush. She called him Roland. And he wondered if he had committed the worst act possible only to end up with the same woman twenty years younger. He felt the bile rising in the back of his throat.

* * *

From behind a rock, Ciaran had seen the man shoot his woman and bury her. He had woken from his nap when he heard the car. Then he watched the man drive away with the window down, smoking a cigarette. Ciarán was no stranger to crime. He'd committed his share of robberies and been involved in more than one scam. He thought of contacting the police, but he didn't know how, and the other Travellers would be mad if he brought attention to the camp. So he kept quiet and told no one what he had witnessed that day. Instead, he made a small spray of wildflowers bound at the stem with a piece of leather tied in a Celtic knot. He placed it carefully in a small crack between the boulders.

* * *

Back at the office, Bodmin put in a call to the Austin Department of Public Safety, where he was connected to the Texas Ranger Division.

"This is DCI John Bodmin from the West Kent police in the UK. I need someone to run a check on a woman named Judith Linnane. I'm not certain if her last address was Austin, Dallas, or Houston."

"Is this Bullhead Bodmin?"

"Yes. Do I know you?"

"No, sir, but I read about the missing McSwayne girl. Everyone knows about that case. Took you years but you finally solved it, congratulations sir."

"Thank you."

"So, what do you need to know about Judith Linnane, Inspector?"

"Anything you can tell me. She's about thirty-five, she's got money, and she's a Sharon Stone look alike."

"I'm on it, sir. Glad to help."

The next day, Bodmin found out that Judith Linnane's husband had died two years earlier in Ireland in an accident at Corcomroe Abbey in The Burren. The unlucky husband had been crushed to death by faulty staging during a reconstruction of the Abbey. The local police had not suspected foul play and felt the widow was genuinely distraught over her husband's death.

Remembering the brochure in Niven's car and believing there is no such thing as coincidence, Bodmin pulled out a map of Ireland and England and began to theorize how Ronald Niven had made it to The Burren, murdered his wife and returned to his estate in Penshurst in less than two days. Once he figured out the route Niven must have used, he boarded a flight to Shannon, where he rented a car and drove north to The Burren.

* * *

He was on his fifth pub and no one had seen anyone who fit the description of Ronald Niven or his wife, Florence. He was tired, hungry, and frustrated.

"Excuse me," he said to the bartender, flashing his credentials, weary of the same introduction.

"I'm DCI John Bodmin with the West Kent police."

"Yes, sir. What can I do for you?"

"I was wondering if you remember a couple who might have eaten here about four days ago. An English couple, tall, distinguished-looking gentleman, and a rather plain-looking woman."

The waiter who was standing by the bar nodded quickly.

"I do."

Bodmin's face lit up.

"The lady was pretty snockered by the time they left. Poor chap had to hold her up to walk."

"I see. Did you overhear any of their conversation by any chance?"

"Well, not that I was eavesdropping, mind you, but I heard the woman complain about going to The Burren."

"I see. Did they say where they were headed in The Burren?"

The bartender paused, thinking. "Yes! The man mentioned Poulnabrone Dolmen. It's a famous tomb just north of here."

"Thank you very much," said Bodmin, bolting out the door.

Bodmin kept heading north and eventually found Poulnabrone Dolmen. He got out of the car and walked around. He scanned the landscape, looking for anything out of the ordinary. A feeling of total isolation enveloped him—as if he were the last person on earth. For over an hour, he walked around the area, not really knowing what he was looking for. Then he got back in the car and drove further into The Burren, where there were larger rocks and boulders.

"Good place to hide a body," he said to no one.

He kept scanning the area, his eyes returning to something that seemed out of place. Then he realized it was a small sprig of wildflowers wedged in the crevice between two boulders. He walked slowly up the hill and saw that the flowers were just starting to wilt. For a few minutes he stood there staring at the flowers, which were tied at the stems in some kind of leather knot.

He looked around again. There wasn't a sound to be heard except for the crunching of his own shoes as he walked. He returned to the rock with the flowers. He looked carefully in and around the large boulder. Then he saw a tiny piece of green tarp sticking out.

An hour later, the body of Florence Denison Niven was discovered. Soon after, Ronald Niven was apprehended at Heathrow Airport, boarding a plane for Corsica with a drunk Judith Linnane.

Niven saw Bodmin at the gate and stopped dead. He took a deep breath and nodded once. And then he held out his hands to be cuffed. It was almost as if he was relieved.

* * *

Every year, when the caravan passed through, Ciarán Devlin placed a small spray of wildflowers in a certain crevice in The Burren. He thought that the body of the woman he had seen murdered still lay beneath. He never knew that it was his kindness and compassion that had inevitably brought Florence Niven's murderer to justice. It was the one piece of the puzzle that DCI Bodmin could never figure out.

Acknowledgements

It is with tremendous gratitude that I express my appreciation to the many people who have helped me in my goal to publish my own collection of short stories. In particular, they are: Anne Bernays, author, for her tough love during my MFA program, Benjamin Percy, author and screenwriter, for his unfailing Rocky-like encouragement during Bread Loaf, Leslie Wheeler, author and editor, and my first supporter at Level Best Books. To Shawn Reilly Simmons, author, editor, and true believer in what I could accomplish, who guided me across the finish line. To my wonderful daughter, Shayne Deal, a constant source of love and reinforcement from the very beginning, and my PR daughter, Natalie Mogauro, who has often been my reader, and doubles as my agent. To my brother, Scott LeBlanc, with the heart of gold, and my sister, Dawn MacCarthy, who once said, "It's not a matter of *if* you can do it, it's a matter of *when* you do it." To my dearest friends, Frances Mitchell, Diane Holbrook, Pat Gonda, and Jean Dyer, whose support means the world to me, and to Sharon Jackson Bailey my steadfast retailer. To Dr. Pat D'Amore, my close friend, who read my very first drafts and told me, "You are my favorite writer, waiting in the wings." To Drs. Diane Bielenberg and Magali Saint-Geniez, who have always attended the important events in my writing journey.

Most importantly, to my husband, Peter Bagley, without whom I would never have received my MFA, attended Bread Loaf, or had the confidence to keep on trying no matter how many rejections I received. You are everything good in my life, and I love you more than words can say...

About the Author

Christine Bagley publishes short stories in both crime anthologies and literary journals. She holds a Master's Degree in Creative Writing from Lesley University in Cambridge, and was a fiction contributor to the Bread Loaf Writers' Conference. She also taught writing and presentation skills to Harvard Medical School foreign national scientists and physicians. The former co-editor and co-publisher of Crime Spell Books, Bagley's stories have appeared in Briar Cliff Review, Bryant Literary Review, Untoward Magazine, Fiction on the Web in the UK, and in multiple editions of Best New England Crime Stories. A finalist for the Al Blanchard Award for Short Crime Fiction, her stories encompass character-driven literary fiction, with shades of dark humor and the supernatural, that draw the reader into her protagonists' inner world and turmoil.

In her spare time, Bagley enjoys writing book reviews, walking, reading, and swimming in any beach she can find. Throughout the year, she attends national and international tennis tournaments. She is a member of Mystery Writers of America, Sisters in Crime New England, and the Short Mystery Fiction Society.

AUTHOR WEBSITE:

www.christinebagley.com

SOCIAL MEDIA HANDLE:

Facebook